**'You don't wan
you?' Ludovic**

'Admit what?'

'That you were restless for the same reason as I was.'

'I don't know why you couldn't sleep.'

'Yes, you do. Women know instinctively when a man's attracted to them, even if he tries not to show it. . .which I haven't.'

She found herself whirled to face him, both his arms firmly round her.

'You don't seriously think I'm going to let you escape without even kissing you, do you?'

Anne Weale was still at school when a women's magazine published some of her stories. At twenty-five she had her first novel accepted by Mills & Boon. Now, with a grown-up son and still happily married to her first love, Anne divides her life between her winter home, a Spanish village ringed by mountains and vineyards, and a summer place in Guernsey, one of the many islands around the world she has used as backgrounds for her books.

NEVER GO BACK

BY
ANNE WEALE

MILLS & BOON
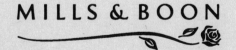

*MILLS & BOON and the Rose Device
are trademarks of the publisher.
Harlequin Mills & Boon Limited,
Eton House, 18–24 Paradise Road, Richmond, Surrey TW9 1SR
This edition published by arrangement with
Harlequin Enterprises B.V.*

© Anne Weale 1995

ISBN 0 263 79331 1

*Set in 10 on 12 pt Linotron Times
01-9512-53626*

*Typeset in Great Britain by CentraCet, Cambridge
Made and printed in Great Britain*

CHAPTER ONE

IT WAS Olivia's habit, whenever she came home after an evening out, to check for messages on her answering-machine.

Tonight, preoccupied with the not unexpected but still rather upsetting ending of a long relationship, she nearly forgot her routine. When she did remember, the message awaiting her was far more of a shock than the break-up with her now ex-boyfriend.

The recorded voice was one she hadn't heard for years but would have recognised instantly, even if the message hadn't begun with the speaker's name.

'Good evening, Miss Hartley. This is Ludovic Webb of Ramillies College. You've been recommended to us as a talented decorator—a specialist in the refurbishment of old houses. The college is planning renovations and we need the advice of someone with your qualifications. If you're interested, please call me as soon as possible to arrange an appointment.'

In the authoritative voice which had once dismissed her from his presence—but she doubted if he would remember that humiliation—Ludovic Webb gave and repeated his telephone number.

She wondered how he had obtained her private number.

There had been a time when she would have preferred to go bankrupt rather than work for him. But if time had not lessened her passionate dislike, it had taught her that no commissions could be rejected out of hand in a decade when almost everyone in her profession had been through a tough time riding out the recession. When a boom was followed by a downturn, interior decoration was a service people could and did do without.

To be approached by the man at the helm of an enterprise like Ramillies College was a piece of luck all her competitors would envy her. She wasn't about to throw it back in his teeth, however much she might want to in her private persona.

Anyway, it was more than likely that several of her colleagues would also be summoned to the college. She would have to compete for the commission, and hope that Ludovic wouldn't connect the sophisticated woman of twenty-eight with the hot-headed, angry nineteen-year-old who had stormed at him long ago.

She went through to her bedroom. When she wasn't preoccupied, it gave her a buzz of pleasure every time she entered it. With its four-poster bed, patchwork quilt and comfortably cushioned *chaise longue*, the room was the fulfilment of a teenage dream from the years when, in winter, she had spent a lot of her free time curled up on the shelf above the huge copper hot-water tank in Mr Rathbone Webb's bathroom at Ramillies.

The eccentric old man had lived on his own in the great house, looked after by his butler-cum-general factotum George Jones and a cleaning woman from the village. Olivia had grown up at Ramillies and had loved every inch of the house and the surrounding estate.

But, when she was seventeen, old Mr Webb and George, her grandfather, had decided it was time for her to see the world. Mr Webb had arranged for her to go as an au pair to a young couple whose grand-parents had been friends of his long ago.

And so, unwillingly, Olivia had been transported to a beautiful house on Cape Cod, whose owners were very rich and lived in the height of luxury with their sheets and towels changed every day and the most delicious food she had ever tasted.

Mr Webb and her grandfather had eaten a lot of chops and sausages, but young Mrs Tyler Westmacott—Bonnie to her friends—had been extremely health-conscious. She and her family had lived on seafood and salads and gallons of freshly squeezed orange juice. Very soon Olivia—called Olly by the Westmacott children—had begun to lose weight. The spots which had plagued her since puberty had started to clear.

Remembering that gradual metamorphosis from a shy, self-conscious late developer into the out-going and confident girl she had become during her time with the Westmacotts, Olivia thought how lucky she was to have had that unforgettable year under Bonnie's wing.

Without it, she could never have become a success-ful career woman.

But not so successful in my private life, she thought wryly, as she entered her bedroom to undress.

Tonight, to have dinner with Mark at one of the fashionable restaurants where he liked to be seen, she had added a silk chiffon scarf to the collarless neckline of her simple but elegant suit and anchored the scarf on her shoulder with an unusual gold brooch.

Mark, one of the youngest Members of Parliament in the House of Commons, was already beginning to show the signs of the rich living he enjoyed. Olivia didn't have his weight problem, partly because she was more physically active and also because he always chose the richest dishes and she the lighter, less fattening ones.

It was a shared desire to get on in the world which had drawn them together. They had both come from humble beginnings and were driven by a fierce ambition to reach the top of their respective spheres.

Still slightly jet-lagged from the flight back from California, and worried about a meeting with her accountant tomorrow, Olivia hadn't really wanted to have dinner with Mark tonight. And she hadn't been looking forward to going back to his flat to make love. Sex with Mark had lost its excitement some time ago.

So it had been with a mixture of relief and regret that she had agreed to his suggestion that they should call it a day.

'I've known for some time that you were never going to be happy as a parliamentary wife,' he had told her. 'I'm not sure you wanted to be married at all, and an MP's wife has to be especially supportive.'

Perhaps he was right. Perhaps, being absorbed in her career, she wasn't cut out for marriage.

After she had hung up her clothes, she put on a nightdress and took her bra, briefs and tights to the bathroom to soak in the basin while she creamed off her make-up.

She had once consulted a make-up expert who had listed her good and bad points: the assets being her large grey eyes, the shape of her mouth, and the texture and sheen of the thick fair hair she was currently wearing brushed back from her forehead and temples in a casual but well-cut bob.

When she was ready for bed, instead of selecting a

book from the stack on her bedside table, she put out the light and lay down. An early night would banish the last trace of tiredness after the crowded schedule of the trip to California.

As she waited for sleep to come she didn't think about Mark. That phase of her life was over. There was nothing to be gained by holding a mental post mortem. What she needed to focus her mind on was how to drum up more business if, tomorrow, the session with her accountant was as bad, or only marginally less worrying, than the previous conference with him.

Inevitably, this turned her thoughts to the message on her answering-machine and the re-entry into her life of the man who, a long time ago, had caused her so many sleepless nights.

Olivia telephoned Ramillies at nine-fifteen the next morning. She had been up since six, starting the day with a shower followed by her daily exercises and a light breakfast of muesli and fruit. Then she had done a couple of hours' work in the studio. This had been the flat's second bedroom but, having no family and no intimate friends outside London, she had little use for a visitors' room.

The number given her by Ludovic was not the one she had dialled when calling home from the other side of the world during the year she and another girl had spent backpacking on both sides of the Pacific. In those days the telephone had been answered by one or other of the two old men who had been her family. Now the voice of a switchboard operator said briskly, 'Ramillies College. Good morning?'

'Good morning. Last night I received a request to call Mr Webb. My name is Olivia Hartley.'

'One moment please, Miss Hartley.' A pause. 'You're through to Mr Webb now.'

'Good morning, Miss Hartley.' The deep voice, now speaking live into her ear, brought back a memory which made Olivia's lips tighten.

But her own voice was calm and courteous as she answered, 'Good morning, Mr Webb. Thank you for your message. When would it be convenient for us to meet?'

'I have to be in London tomorrow. Is your diary already full?'

'No, I have some spaces in it. If you'd like to come to my office in Walton Street, I can show you some previous commissions which have similarities with Ramillies.'

'Have you been to Ramillies before?' he asked.

She avoided a direct answer. 'Since you turned the house into a college it's become very well-known. I've read several features about it in newspapers and magazines. Tomorrow I'm free from eleven to noon, and after half-past three.'

'Late afternoon would suit me best. Is five-thirty too late for you?'

'Five-thirty would be fine.' She gave him the full address and her office telephone number in case he needed to contact her the following day. 'By the way, who gave you my home number?' she asked.

'The custodian at Hertington Castle. I don't like everything that's been done to the place since it's been opened as a conference centre, but I strongly approved of the rooms I was told you'd designed.'

'Thank you. I'm glad you liked them. I'll see you tomorrow then, Mr Webb.'

They exchanged goodbyes and she rang off, a slight frown contracting her eyebrows.

What if he did recognise her? Would their previous encounter wreck her chances of wresting this plum commission from her rivals?

Her mind went back to the day she had returned to Ramillies to find everything changed. . .

Catching sight of her reflection in a glass door at the station, Olly—as she was used to being called now—wondered what she would have been like if she had stayed at home these past two years. Still one hundred and fifty-three pounds and plagued by pimples, probably.

Instead of which her weight was down to one hundred and nineteen pounds and the unsightly zits, as American teenagers called them, were a thing of the past. And those weren't the only changes her two old darlings would see in her. She was fitter, as well as slimmer, and her long, untidy hair was now a short, sun-bleached cap of silky-soft bristles. They wouldn't like the punk hairstyle, and she didn't mean to keep it that way, but it was practical for backpacking and she counterbalanced the butch effect by always wearing the silver ear-rings Tom had given her in Bali.

Remembering that beautiful island and the happiness of her first love-affair, with a boy from New Zealand, a reminiscent smile curled her mouth. 'Kiwi' the others had called him, but his real name had been Thomas, and a nicer guy she could never hope to meet. But basically it had been a loving friendship, not the start of 'till death us do part'.

Now Tom was back on his father's sheep station in New Zealand's North Island, and very soon she would be back at Ramillies, where she belonged.

As the buses which passed the estate were few and far between, Olly headed for the taxi rank outside the station building.

'Where d'you want to go, miss?' the driver asked as he heaved her laden pack into the boot.

She gave him the name of the small village close to her home. 'Shall I sit in front with you? I've been away a long time. You can fill me in on what's been happening around here.'

'Not much,' the driver said drily. 'Where've you been?'

'All kinds of places. But there's nowhere like home. I can't wait to get back,' she said, smiling.

Mr Webb and Granpa didn't know it yet, but from now on she was going to take care of them, repay those two dear old men for all the years they had looked after her.

'I don't often go to Lynchet Parva,' said the driver, as they left the station-yard and headed in the opposite direction from the centre of the large market town where Olly's school clothes and shoes had been bought for her.

'The last fare I took there was someone from London going to a funeral,' he added. 'I reckon it must have been one of the biggest funerals they've ever had in that little church.'

There were several rich, important people living in the vicinity of the village, Olly remembered. Some of them had tried to make friends with Mr Webb, but he hadn't wanted to know them.

He had been a sociable man once, but not since the

Second World War. He had survived the conflict, in spite of being on active service for five years. But his eighteen-year-old son had been shot down during the Battle of Britain and while Rathbone—then a much-decorated colonel—had been campaigning in Italy, his wife, doing war-work in London, had died in an air raid.

'Whose funeral was it?' Olly asked.

'Some old boy who lived in a big house with a foreign-sounding name. Nearly ninety, he was, so my fare was telling me. You'd think everyone who knew him would be dead and gone, but no end of people turned out. There was a photograph of the house and a write-up in the local paper. He'd given a lot of money to charities and they all sent someone down. In fact, from what I've heard since, he gave so much away, there's nothing left to keep the place up.'

Olly felt as if someone had kicked her in the stomach. In the faint hope that she had misunderstood him, or the driver had got it wrong, she said hoarsely, 'Was the house called Ramillies?'

'That's it. . . Ramillies. He wasn't a foreigner himself. His surname was Webb. But his first name was something peculiar. I've forgotten it now.'

'Rathbone.'

'You're right. . . Rathbone. Knew him, did you? By name, if not to speak to?'

'I knew him very well. My grandfather is. . .was his butler. When was the funeral?'

'About six weeks ago. I expect your family thought the news would keep till you came home. It was only to be expected at his age, wasn't it?'

'I suppose so,' she murmured hollowly. But she hadn't expected it. The Webbs were a long-lived family. She had expected to find Rathbone as active, short-tempered and sardonically humorous as he had been when she left. She couldn't believe she would never see him again.

'Why was the house called Ramillies?' asked the driver. 'Did he have foreign ancestors?'

'It's the name of a village in Belgium where a great battle was fought. You've heard of Blenheim Palace?'

He nodded. 'I've been there. My wife likes going round stately 'omes. I'm not that keen, myself, but she and our daughter like it. I was quite interested to see the room where Sir Winston Churchill was born.' After a pause, he added, 'But from what I remember of the photo, Ramillies isn't a quarter the size of Blenheim. That really is a palace.'

Olly had also been to Blenheim, on a day-trip from school in the charge of their history teacher.

She said, 'Blenheim was a gift from Queen Anne to John Churchill, first Duke of Marlborough. It was a reward for his victories paid for by the nation. The Webb who fought under Marlborough's command at Ramillies paid for his house out of his own pocket.'

She could have gone on to tell him how the house had been enlarged by successive generations, their piecemeal additions in the style of their day adding to Ramillies' charm and character, but she was not in the mood. It was he who continued to talk about the various stately homes he and his family had visited at weekends, while Olly sat in shattered silence.

On the outskirts of Lynchet Parva, she directed him to drop her by a gate in the boundary wall from which there was a short-cut between the house and the village. Even Mr Webb had never used the imposing main gateway. For as long as she could remember it had been locked and padlocked.

She was walking along the path across the park, her throat thick with unshed tears for the old man she had loved as much, if not more, than her biological grandfather, when she saw a tall man striding towards her. She had never seen him before, yet something about him was oddly familiar.

'Hello. . .where are you going?' he asked, when they were within speaking distance.

Before going to America, Olly had seldom encountered any very tall people, apart from old Mr Webb who, by the time she knew him, had become stooped and arthritic. Now she was used to seeing men whose height was well over six feet. But usually they were great beefy hulks, or as lankily built as giraffes. This man's body was in perfect proportion to his height, with broad shoulders set off by a blue chambray shirt and long, lean legs in a clean pair of dark blue jeans.

'To the house. Where else?' she said, wondering who he was. His colouring was more Latin than Anglo-Saxon: his hair as dark as it came, short of being the true black of Indian and Asian hair, and his skin deeply tanned. But his eyes were the colour of his indigo jeans.

'The house isn't open to the public. Nor are there any camping facilities in the grounds. What made you think there might be?' he asked.

His voice made him hard to place. He didn't have a local accent, but nor did he sound like Rathbone—or George Jones. When talking to his employer, her grandfather had always spoken in a carefully posh voice. Alone with Olly, he reverted to the speech of his native London, larded with words she was forbidden to use.

'I live here,' she answered brusquely, in no mood to talk to strangers.

His immediate reaction was to arch a sceptical eyebrow, at the same time scanning her appearance for any details not tagged during his first comprehensive appraisal of her face and figure.

Then his expression changed. 'Is your name Jones?'

It wasn't, but she didn't bother to correct a widespread misconception that her name was the same as her grandfather's.

'I'm Mr Jones's granddaughter,' she acknowledged. 'Who are you?'

'Rathbone Webb's great-nephew. He died at the beginning of last month, leaving the house to his next of kin—myself. My name's Ludovic Webb. And yours is——?' As he asked, he held out his hand.

'Olly.' It was so long since anyone had called her by her given name that she no longer thought of herself as Olivia. Taking the hand he offered, she said, 'The taxi driver told me about Mr Webb dying. Had you ever met him?'

Ludovic Webb shook his head. 'He and his younger brother didn't get on and my father was raised overseas. This is my first visit to Ramillies, although not my first time in England.'

Aware of the latent strength in the large tanned hand holding hers, Olly repeated the question she had asked and been asked innumerable times during her travels. 'Where are you from?'

'A difficult question to answer. I was born at sea, in the Mozambique Channel. I've no close links with any particular piece of land. . .or hadn't, until I inherited this ancient ruin.' He waved a hand in the direction of the house.

'It isn't a ruin,' she said indignantly. 'It's a beautiful house. It just needs some money spent on it.'

'Unfortunately there isn't any. What there was has been given away. Having no direct descendants, Rathbone wasn't bothered about conserving his fortune for whoever came after him. The estate will have to be sold.'

The idea of Ramillies being sold was almost as brutal a shock as the taxi driver's announcement of Rathbone's death.

'You can't sell it!' she exclaimed, horrified.

'Without the means to keep it, I have no option,' he answered, with a dismissive shrug. 'Where have you come from?'

'I landed at Heathrow airport first thing this morning. . .from Miami. This time yesterday morning I was in Guatemala.'

'You'll be glad to have a shower and get changed.'

'Yes. . .after I've seen my grandfather. How is he taking it. . . Mr Webb's death?' she asked, realising it was Ludovic's intention to return to the house with her.

'He's bearing up.'

'Had Mr Webb been ill?'

'I'm told not. He was in his usual good health right up to the night he died. . .in his sleep. But it wasn't exactly unexpected. He was in his eighty-ninth year.'

'All the same, it will have hit Granpa very hard. He's looked after Mr Webb for nearly forty years. He'll be lost without him. If I'd known, I'd have come back at once.'

Although she was walking briskly, with his much

longer legs the man beside her was moving at little
more than a comfortable stroll.

Suddenly, glancing up at him, she realised why he
had seemed familiar. Although his colouring was different from the fair-haired grey-eyed people in the
many family portraits at Ramillies, he had the aquiline
nose and thrusting chin common to most of the male
Webbs.

She wondered how old he was. It was hard to judge.
His physique was as taut and muscular as Tom's
twenty-year-old body had been. But there were fine
lines fanning from the outer corners of the dark blue
eyes.

'Do you still live at sea?' she asked.

He looked down at her. 'Some of the time, yes.
Done any crewing on your travels?'

Olly shook her head. 'We were once offered berths
on a schooner, but we didn't take them. The friend I
was travelling with didn't like the look of the skipper.'

'Was your friend male or female?'

'Female.'

'She was right to be wary. Even with two of you, a
lecherous skipper can make a pest of himself. . .
Unless you have the know-how to get the boat back to
port after you've clonked him on the head and trussed
him up,' he added, amusement deepening the lines she
had noticed. 'I once knew a girl who did that, but she
was older than you and had been around boats all her
life. How long have you been away from here?'

'Two years.'

Suddenly her eyes filled with tears. This was so
different from the happy home-coming she had
expected. She averted her face so that he shouldn't see

how upset she was. She didn't want to cry in front of a stranger, especially this one.

How could he understand what Ramillies meant to her? He didn't know its history, and the stories attached to all its contents. To him it was just a relic of a privileged way of life which was fast disappearing.

To her relief he didn't ask any more questions. By the time they reached the house she had her emotions under precarious control.

They entered by way of a side-door, which Ludovic unlocked with a key from a bunch attached by a chain to his belt and kept in the pocket of his jeans.

'Considering theft is a growing industry these days, it's amazing a house with such minimal security arrangements hasn't been stripped long before this,' he remarked, as he pushed the door open for her. 'Tomorrow a team from Bonaby's, the fine arts auctioneers, are coming to inventory the contents. Meanwhile I've engaged a couple of security guards to patrol the place at night until the sale of the contents is over.'

'You're not going to sell all the family heirlooms as well?' she exclaimed, aghast.

'Without the house, what am I supposed to do with them? There's enough stuff in here to fill a couple of repositories. I shall keep a few things. Incidentally, Rathbone has left you one or two keepsakes. I gather he was fond of you.'

'It was mutual,' Olly said thickly. 'He was a dear. . . It's a shame you never met him.'

'That's not how I've heard him described by others around here,' Ludovic commented drily.

'Not many people knew him. All the time I've lived here he's never been outside the grounds, and not many people were given permission to come in. But if he heard of local people in trouble he always helped them.' As she spoke, she took off her pack and dumped it on the floor of the passage which led to the heart of the house, the Great Hall. 'Have you any idea where I'll find my grandfather?'

'He's not here.'

'Not here? What do you mean? Where is he?' Olly queried anxiously.

'Don't panic, he's fine. You can see him this afternoon.' Ludovic lifted the pack by its shoulder-straps. 'This is a heavy load for a girl of your build to carry.' He led the way down the passage, taking the pack with him.

'I don't understand. Why can't I see him now?'

'Because you don't have a car, and it isn't convenient for me to run you there now,' he said over his shoulder. 'Anyway, you need to freshen up. You've been in transit for around thirty hours. . .and it shows.'

'How far away is he? *Where* is he?' Olly demanded.

'He's in a snug little flat in a complex of sheltered housing for elderly people about ten miles from here. It was lucky they had a vacancy. They also have two or three bedrooms for the use of residents' visitors. You can stay there for several nights, until you've decided what you're going to do next.'

These announcements, delivered in the arbitrary tone of someone accustomed to having his arrangements and decisions accepted without argument or even comment, left Olly temporarily stupefied.

She couldn't imagine anything her grandfather would dislike more than being bundled off to an old people's home, where he would have to conform to all sorts of rules and regulations.

However, by the time she had recovered sufficiently to point this out, they had turned away from the Great Hall and arrived at the kitchen. At the scrubbed deal table in the centre of it a woman she didn't know was trimming the pasty overlapping a baking dish.

'Mrs Oakes, this is Olly Jones, whose grandfather looked after my great-uncle. Would you take her up to my room and run a bath for her? If she wants to press any clothes, give her an iron and a board, please.' Ludovic glanced at his watch before turning to Olly. 'I was on my way to the post when we ran into each other. I can still make the one o'clock collection. I'll be back in about half an hour. Save your questions for lunch.'

As he was turning away he said, as an afterthought, 'If you have a skirt or a dress in your pack, it might help the old man to recognise you. He showed me a snap taken before you left here. I didn't recognise you as his granddaughter, and I shouldn't think he will either. Also, people of his age don't take kindly to lavatory brush haircuts.'

With a mocking flash of very white teeth, he left the kitchen.

'Well, I never! That's telling you straight, isn't it?' said Mrs Oakes, after a pause. 'Still, I've heard the same thing said about the old gentleman. . .that he was very outspoken.'

Inwardly, Olly was furious. Both at Ludovic's dictatorial attitude and his reference to the photograph he had seen. Even now she was not photogenic, and in her last year at school had been even less so. The passport photograph, which must be the snap he had seen of her, had been taken a few days before her period, when her spots were always at their worst. She

had looked like a currant bun. Only this morning, a
young immigration official had given her an interested
look as she stepped up to his desk and then, after
glancing at her passport, had said quizzically, 'You
should get this picture updated. It doesn't flatter you.'

She had laughed and blushed, not much minding
that he had seen her at her teenage worst. But somehow it was far more galling for Ludovic Webb to be
privy to the mess she had been at seventeen.

She went down to lunch, refreshed by her bath but
still simmering at the high-handed way her grandfather
had been shunted into accommodation he wouldn't
like and which wasn't what old Mr Webb had promised
would be provided for him.

Deliberately, she had ignored Ludovic's advice, and
was wearing a clean shirt and jeans instead of the
crumpled chinos she had travelled in. There was a skirt
in her pack, for travelling in places where trousers and
shorts on women were unacceptable. But she was
damned if she'd wear it on Ludovic's say-so.

At present the house was exactly as she remembered
it. But tomorrow it would be invaded by the auctioneers. She hated to think of them prying into every
nook and corner for items of value.

If it were mine, I would fight tooth and nail to keep
everything together, she thought, pausing halfway
down the staircase to gaze at the portrait of a girl in an
Edwardian ball-dress—Rathbone Webb's mother. She
was also one of Ludovic's forebears. How could he let
her be sold off to some rich yuppie as an 'instant
ancestress'?

On the wall of the next flight, hanging in a sloping
line, were photographs of Rathbone in the days when
he had been 'Tiger' Webb, a subaltern in the Punjabi

Irregular Frontier Force, keeping the north-west frontier of India safe for travellers and traders.

Pictures of him and his young brother officers, dashing in regimental turbans or dressed for polo and pig-sticking, filled the numerous albums he had shown her to illustrate tales of hunting jackal with hounds sent from England and other exotic pursuits.

But while 'Tiger' had finished his military career a colonel, after winning many decorations for valour, his younger brother—the grandfather of the man with whom she was about to eat—had been a ne'er-do-well, whose expulsion from school had led to other disgraces. Eventually he had been given an allowance, on condition he went far away and brought no more shame on his family. She wouldn't be surprised if some of his unpleasant propensities had been transmitted to his grandson.

Mrs Oakes had told her lunch would be served in the library, but Olly had no time to enjoy the atmosphere of this dearly loved room where so many happy hours of her childhood had been passed. Ludovic was there before her, sitting on top of the wheeled ladder where she herself had often perched.

As she closed the door behind her, he shut the book he'd been reading, replaced it on the top shelf and, without touching the handrail, walked down the steps with the ease of a man accustomed to steep companion ladders.

CHAPTER TWO

'DID your two aged mentors teach you to share their appreciation of wine?' he asked.

Olly shook her head. She knew Rathbone had been a connoisseur who, every night, with his dinner, had drunk a bottle of fine wine and smoked an expensive cigar. But although it was he who had taught her to love books, he had discouraged her from smoking and drinking. Indeed, he had promised her that, if she kept clear of both habits while she was away, when she came back from her travels there would be a very special reward for her.

She had often been tempted to experiment, but her wish to keep his good opinion and her curiosity about the unspecified reward had been more effective than the pressure of her peers to conform.

'It was a strange upbringing for you. . .alone in this mausoleum with two decrepit old men. But I expect you made up for lost time while you were in the States,' said Ludovic, crossing the room to a Regency breakfast table now set for lunch for two.

'In some ways—yes,' she agreed. 'But I was very happy here. *You* may see this as a mausoleum, but *I* think it's a wonderful house. And they weren't decrepit when I left. They were old, but I like old people. When they're as wise and funny and kind as Mr Webb was,' she added.

Ludovic had drawn out one of the chairs at the table and was waiting for her to be seated. That he should have the same courtly manners as his great-uncle was unexpected.

As he moved to his place opposite her, she took the limp damask napkin from the side-plate and unfolded it across her lap. While her grandfather had been in charge the napkins had always been starched, and she could remember the helpers who had done the washing and ironing complaining to each other about what a fusspot he was.

As it had on the way to the house, a choking lump filled her throat, and it was a relief when Mrs Oakes came in, pushing a trolley and distracting Ludovic's attention from the fact that his unexpected and no doubt unwelcome guest was again on the brink of tears.

On the top shelf of the trolley was a tureen of pale green chilled soup, an artistically arranged platter of chicken salad and a bottle of wine in a cooler. Below was an apple tart, a dish of whipped cream and a plug-in coffee percolator.

'Mrs Oakes is an excellent cook,' said Ludovic, after she had served the soup and left the room. He offered Olly a basket of fragrant hot rolls.

'Where did you find her?' she asked.

'She keeps house for friends of mine in London. As they're away for some weeks, I asked if I could borrow her. I don't mind roughing it at sea, but when I'm ashore I like to be comfortable and well-fed.'

'Where's your boat at the moment?'

'I've left her in the Caribbean. Were the West Indies on your itinerary?'

Olly shook her head. 'We wanted to see the less touristy places. . .not beaches full of basting bodies.'

'On the boat you can bypass those beaches and find

moorings the tourists can't reach. How did you pay for your travels? Did your grandfather put up the money?'

'No, your great-uncle did. But I didn't ask him to. I was living as an au pair with an American family and they had some older friends whose daughter wanted to travel. Her parents were worried about her going on her own and I was chosen to go with her. I didn't ask Mr Webb to finance the trip. It was all arranged over my head.'

'I see. What's next on your agenda?'

'I was going to take over my grandfather's job. . .let him retire while I ran the house for them both.'

'No other career plans?' Ludovic asked, filling their water-glasses from a jug of iced water.

'Not as long as I was needed here.'

'In the nature of things, my great-uncle couldn't have gone on much longer. What were you planning to do then?'

'I hadn't looked that far ahead. I'd done what they wanted me to—seen the world, had some adventures. I assumed I'd be needed here for some time. Mr Webb promised my grandfather that, if he died first, we could have the lodge cottage for the rest of Granpa's life.'

'Did he? Well, he was very old, and perhaps not in full possession of his faculties. The lodge will have to be sold with the rest of the estate. Your grandfather is better off where he is, and you need to earn your living somewhere with more opportunities than this part of the world has to offer. Did you do well at school?'

'Not specially.' Olly had the feeling he didn't believe her about the cottage.

'What was your best subject?'

'I wasn't outstanding at anything.' She could have

added that she hadn't discovered her *métier* until after she had left school and that, when she was free to pursue it, Bonnie Westmacott had promised to pull some strings for her. But in the face of Ludovic's sceptical attitude she didn't feel inclined to confide her dreams and aspirations.

'In that case your best bet is to acquire some computer skills,' he told her. 'A girl who can handle a word-processor, spreadsheet and database can always find a job. I'm prepared to finance a crash-course in those skills to give you a start. But after that, it's up to you.'

'Thank you, but that won't be necessary,' Olly said stiffly. 'The way things are now, I'd rather be independent. Granpa has savings. We don't need any handouts.'

He looked at her with an expression she couldn't interpret. Instinct told her that, although he had gone through the motions of receiving her kindly, his manner was a front for other feelings, that, for some reason she couldn't fathom, her return was both inconvenient and annoying.

While she was helping herself to the salad, he took the bottle from the cooler. It had already been opened by Mrs Oakes and he only had to remove the loosened cork. But before he could fill her glass, Olly put her hand over it.

'Not for me, thank you.' She wasn't about to try her first glass of wine in the company of someone she didn't altogether trust.

He didn't press her to change her mind. After filling his own glass, he said, 'Maybe he didn't before, but now your grandfather sleeps after lunch. We'll go over there about four, which will give you time to stretch your legs in the park.'

Olly's appetite was geared to a time-zone six hours behind UK time and she was still feeling full from all the meals served in-flight. She managed to finish her small helping of salad, but couldn't cope with the tart.

Not surprisingly for so tall a man, Ludovic had a hearty appetite, and added three large spoonfuls of cream to his generous slice of tart as if he had never heard of the hazards of animal fats. But with no spare flesh on his body, and plenty of well-developed muscle, he looked set to emulate his great-uncle in the longevity stakes.

While he ate, and Olly drank water to correct the dehydration of the long hours in the air, he questioned her on her travels.

He seemed to have been almost everywhere she and Kate had been. In different circumstances, she would have enjoyed comparing notes with him. But Mr Webb's death and her grandfather's removal from Ramillies drained the pleasure from everything, even being back in this room, with the sun slanting on the faded cushions on the window-seat and the familiar panorama of low, sheep-cropped hills and peaceful woods to be seen through the window.

'How can you let all this go?' she burst out suddenly, interrupting what he was saying about Fiji. 'How can you throw away the heritage of centuries?'

Ludovic leaned back in his chair, his long fingers resting lightly on the stem of his wine-glass.

He said coldly, 'It's not *my* heritage. . .and you need to be reminded that it isn't yours either. That may be why Rathbone sent you away. . .because he could see you were becoming too wrapped up in the place. I'm surprised you still feel possessive about it. Your two years overseas should have cleared your head of all that adolescent nonsense. The real world has a lot more to offer than this white elephant.'

Olly felt an upsurge of anger which threatened to overwhelm all the normal restraints of good manners. For the first time in her life, she understood why people committed murders and crimes of passion. There was something about this man's implacable attitude which made her long to snatch up her glass of water and dash its contents in his unyielding face.

Instead, she said stiffly, 'Excuse me,' and rose from the table.

Ludovic also rose and, because of his long stride, arrived at the door ahead of her. His punctilious courtesy in opening it for her was the final exasperation. She managed to contain her temper only by a whisker. As soon as she heard the door close, she started to run, tearing through the house and then, once outside, across the neglected garden to a secret place where she could vent her feelings of rage and despair. . .

She was startled out of the deep sleep of emotional and physical exhaustion by having her face licked by an elderly black Labrador.

Olly had forgotten about Jack, the last of a long line of gun-dogs bred at Ramillies. She flung her arms round his neck, thankful it was he and not Ludovic who had found her sleeping off a storm of tears which must have left tell-tale streaks on her face.

Crying wasn't her style. But until today nothing seriously bad had ever happened to her. It was the combination of her first experience of grief combined with the fatigue of the journey from Guatemala which had reduced her to tears.

Breaking off her affectionate reunion with the grey-muzzled dog to look at her watch, she saw that it was half-past three. She had better sneak back to the house and wash her face before Ludovic saw her. She could imagine his thinly veiled scorn for what he would no doubt regard as childish behaviour.

With Jack padding at her heels, his tail swinging happily at finding someone familiar still around, she returned to the house.

'What are you going to do about Jack?' she asked when, half an hour later, she was sitting beside Ludovic in a dark green Range Rover which might, like Mrs Oakes, have been lent by his London friends.

'Jack who?'

'Mr Webb's dog. . .the Labrador.'

'Oh. . .the dog. How old is he? Nearly as old as you, by the look of his muzzle.'

'He's fourteen, but there's nothing wrong with him. I'm sure someone would give him a home. He's very gentle and affectionate. . .ideal with children.'

Don't say he's got to be put down. I couldn't bear it, she thought.

But what Ludovic said was, 'He's the least of my worries,' and she thought it wiser to let the subject drop and hope that she could find someone who would want to give Jack a home. She would herself. . .if she had somewhere to go where pets were allowed.

The place where her grandfather was living was much as she had expected: a purpose-built complex of neat bungalows, with a communal garden shared by the occupants of a two-storey central block of apartments, and the warden's office just inside the entrance.

Ludovic introduced her to the warden's wife and explained that Olly would need a bed for a few nights.

'No problem. All our guest-rooms are free this week and next. Mr Jones will be ever so pleased to see you, dear. He's been very down, poor old chap. Wait a minute, I'll give him a call.' She switched on a Tannoy, pressed one of a row of buttons and, raising her voice, said, 'Are you awake, Mr Jones?'

There was a pause and what sounded like muttered curses before a man's voice said irritably, 'I am now! What do you want?'

'There's a visitor for you. A young lady. Can you guess who? I'll bring her up straight away.'

Carrying Olly's pack, Ludovic followed them up the staircase and along the wide corridor between the numbered doors of the flats. But when they reached number nine, he put the pack down and said goodbye.

'Such a nice, helpful man,' Mrs Green said approvingly, watching him disappearing down the stairs.

Olly wondered if Ludovic thought he had now seen the last of her. She certainly had no wish to prolong their acquaintance, but at the same time she wasn't going to stand meekly by while he deprived her grandfather of his entitlements.

When the door was opened by a scowling old man in pyjamas and carpet slippers, she was shocked by the change in him.

And it wasn't until she opened her arms and stepped forward, saying, 'Granpa. . . I'm back!' that his expression changed into a smile of delighted disbelief.

The following afternoon, refreshed by a good night's sleep in a comfortable bed and while her grandfather was having his post-lunch nap, she borrowed a bicycle and rode back to Ramillies, determined not to let

Ludovic get away with ignoring the promises made by
his great-uncle.

She now knew slightly more about Ludovic than she
had the day before. Granpa had re-told the story about
Ludovic's grandfather being a black sheep, a disgrace
to the family name, who, eventually, had been given
an allowance and packed off abroad to continue his
dissolute way of life in some distant place where it
wouldn't be an embarrassment.

He would never have been heard of again, except
that many years later his son had written to Rathbone,
asking for financial aid. Previously unaware that he
had a nephew, and delighted to hear of the existence
of an heir, Rathbone had responded with his usual
generosity. He had received little thanks. According
to Granpa, the nephew had refused an invitation to
visit Ramillies and his lack of interest had clouded
Rathbone's last years.

This time Olly entered the estate by the gateway
used by delivery and service vans. This led to the
stable-yard and the entrance leading to the kitchen
and storerooms. However, when she neared the house
she saw that several smart cars were parked there —
the kind of cars which, had the house still been a
family home, would have used the main drive.

Then she remembered that the team of valuers from
Bonaby's had been due to arrive this morning. As she
propped the bike against a wall, she wondered how
many days — perhaps even weeks — it would take them
to inventory the contents of a house in which little had
been discarded since it was built nearly two hundred
and eighty years ago.

There was no one about as she made her way to the
kitchen, where Mrs Oakes was still washing the dishes

from what, judging by the number of glasses, had been an elaborate luncheon for at least six people.

'Can I give you a hand?' Olly offered. She had nothing against Mrs Oakes, and indeed felt rather sorry for her, being expected to provide lavish meals in a kitchen which lacked all mod cons.

'Hello. . . Where have you sprung from?' Mrs Oakes looked surprised, but not displeased to see her.

'I've come to see Ludovic, but I'll dry for you first. I expect you're used to a dishwasher.'

While Olly had been living with the Westmacotts, on Cape Cod and in Boston, Massachusetts, she had discovered how much easier life was with all the up-to-date aids taken for granted by prosperous Americans.

'Yes, but this antique china needs to be washed by hand. A machine might damage the gilding,' said Mrs Oakes, showing her a plate Olly couldn't remember seeing before. 'Mr Webb's very busy today. The men from Bonaby's are here. Could I give him a message and get him to call you back when he's free? Probably not till this evening.'

'It's not something I can discuss on the telephone. I've biked over specially to talk to him. I'm sure he can spare me half an hour. Where will I find him?' asked Olly, crossing the kitchen to fetch a teatowel from the rail on the old-fashioned Aga, installed when such cookers were modern innovations.

'Probably in the library. But I really think it would be better to postpone seeing him until later in the week. He has a lot on his mind and——'

'So have I!' Olly interrupted. 'My grandfather is miserable where he is. To stay there will finish him. Compared with what he's been used to, his flat is as cramped as a rabbit hutch, and he never has a minute's

peace. Either the woman who runs the place is on the
intercom, checking that he's all right, or one of the
widows who lives there is knocking on the door with
something she's cooked for him, or offering to sew on
buttons. I know they all mean to be kind, but he feels
he has no privacy.'

'It's always very hard for old people to adjust to new
circumstances, but I'm sure he'll settle down soon,'
said Mrs Oakes.

Olly shook her head. 'I don't think so. If I'd been
here, he would never have been bundled off there
while he was still in shock over old Mr Webb's death.
He must be turning in his grave,' she added, with
angry emphasis.

'Aren't you being rather unfair to young Mr Webb?'
the other woman suggested. 'What else can he do but
sell up? A great house like this soaks up money like a
sponge.'

'If it were mine, I'd find a way to keep it.'

As soon as the drainer was clear and everything
used at the lunch table had been neatly arranged at
one end of the huge scrubbed deal table, ready for the
following day, Olly left the kitchen to go and confront
her adversary.

For she had no doubt that Ludovic's amiability was
no more than a thin veneer which would rapidly peel
away if she started to make what he would regard as a
nuisance of herself.

In the Great Hall she found a man examining a
Chinese vase.

'Do you know where I'll find Mr Webb?' she asked.

'He's in the library with one of my colleagues.'

'Thank you.'

Bracing herself for the awkwardness of confronting

Ludovic while there was someone else with him, she headed purposefully for the library.

Today she *was* wearing a skirt, with rope-wedged summer shoes which added a couple of inches to her height and a little light make-up. There was nothing to be done about her hair which, according to her grandfather, made her look like 'one of those freaks at the pop music festivals'. She had debated covering it with a scarf tied turban-fashion. But that would have been rather hot for a ten-mile cycle ride on a sunny summer day.

When she knocked on the library door, even Ludovic's answering 'Come in' sounded distinctly unwelcoming.

Olly entered the room, closing the door behind her before crossing to the two men who were sitting at the same table where she had lunched with Ludovic the day before.

'I'm sorry to disturb you when you're busy, but I'm afraid this won't wait,' she said, in a determined voice.

It was the other man who rose first. He was wearing the dark trousers of a city suit but had removed the jacket and was in his shirt-sleeves; the shirt being a dashing affair of brightly striped poplin with a plain white collar and conservative tie.

He was smiling at her. But Ludovic, now also on his feet, was looking decidedly grim.

'This is a most inconvenient time,' he said curtly.

The other man said tactfully, 'I'll go and see how the others are getting on.'

'No, no. . .there's no need to go. This is Olly Jones, the granddaughter of my great-uncle's manservant,' Ludovic told him. He turned to her. 'Mr Hamilton is from Bonaby's and he has an appointment in London at six o'clock,' he added pointedly.

'How do you do, Miss Jones?' The other man gave her a nice smile as they shook hands.

'How do you do?' Olly didn't point out that her surname wasn't Jones. She had more important things on her mind.

Mr Hamilton offered her his chair while he moved to the window-seat.

'What is it you want to see me about?' Ludovic asked her curtly.

'Granpa can't stay in that awful place where you've put him. He's miserable there. It's bad enough losing your closest companion. . . Because he was more than a servant to Mr Webb. They were friends for forty years. He's as devasted as. . .as a wife losing her husband.'

'No one disputes that, Olly. Come to the point.'

'He was promised the cottage. I don't think you have any right to ignore Mr Webb's solemn promise that, if he died first, Granpa could spend the rest of his days at the cottage.'

Ludovic drew a deep breath and immediately exhaled it, in the manner of someone close to the limit of their patience.

'I've already explained that the whole estate has to be sold. It's impossible to exclude the lodge cottage from the sale. If it were somewhere else — in a less important location — that might be different. But situated where it is, next to Ramillies's principal entrance, it has to be included with the house. In any case, the cottage is falling apart. It would need extensive renovations to make it habitable. It's not fit for anyone to live in, let alone an old man in your grandfather's state of health.'

His air of a sensible adult patiently re-explaining something to a rather dim child provoked Olly into retorting, 'You're only looking at the situation from your point of view. You want him out of the way. You want to forget he exists. If I hadn't come back, you'd have got away with it. But I'm back now and I'm not going to let him be. . .incarcerated in that horrible place. *You* wouldn't stay there five minutes. Why should he have to endure it?'

'You're exaggerating,' said Ludovic. 'The apartments are small, but they're perfectly adequate. There are all the facilities he needs, including an excellent meal served every day in the residents' dining-room if he doesn't feel like cooking for himself. Are you sure your indignation about not getting the cottage is not on your own behalf? You've done well out of Ramillies for a long time.' He looked her up and down, his expression sardonic. 'It was too much to hope you could be a Webb dependant forever.'

Olly felt herself turning red with the effort of suppressing the forceful retort which sprang to her lips. Instead she hung on to her temper and kept her voice low and quiet.

'Coming from the heir of an old man whom you never bothered to visit or even write to when he was alive, I think that's a contemptible thing to say. At least I loved Mr Webb, and wrote to him every week while I was in America and later when I was travelling on the allowance he gave me. You aren't even prepared to respect his last wishes.'

Mr Hamilton cleared his throat. 'I think this discussion should continue in private. I'll be in——'

'Stay where you are, please, Hamilton,' Ludovic ordered him sharply. 'If it weren't for your restraining influence, I might give way to the temptation to give this exasperating girl the spanking she ought to have had a long time ago. Which would be a mistake,' he added. 'Not because it wouldn't do her the world of good, but because she would promptly sue.'

'You're not joking!' Olly flashed back. 'I don't know where you've come from, but in this country men can't get away with bullying women any more. Brute strength is out of fashion.'

'Replaced by the collective strength of a monstrous regiment of feminists,' he said acidly. 'I knew you spelt trouble as soon as I saw you, *Ms* Jones. Fortunately, I'm protected from any further intrusions by the law of trespass. You have no right to come here, except by my invitation. If you wish to take this matter further, see my great-uncle's lawyer. Your grandfather knows his address. Now please leave the house. And don't come back.'

Her flush, which had subsided, now swept from her throat to her forehead in a hot tide of impotent chagrin at being made to feel like a harpy.

Not knowing how to deal with the situation, she stood, rooted by embarrassment, until Mr Hamilton stepped forward with a gesture indicating that he would see her to the door.

From the other end of the room, Olly glanced back to where Ludovic had turned away to the window and was standing with his arms folded across his chest. Already, she guessed, he had dismissed her from his mind as effectively as from his presence.

But if he thought he could defeat her as easily as this, he was mistaken. . .

* * *

Olivia gave considerable thought to what to wear for her meeting with Ludovic Webb, nine years after her last sight of him.

She had seen Alistair Hamilton on a number of occasions since then. He was now chairman of Bonaby's and, in that capacity, had several times shaken hands with her at receptions and special exhibitions put on by the famous auction-house. Olivia had been present because she subscribed to several of Bonaby's catalogues and often bought things at auction. But she knew Alistair didn't connect her with the girl he had met at Ramillies, and she was reasonably confident that Ludovic wouldn't recognise her either.

Nevertheless, she spent the day in a rather jittery state, which she told herself was because being selected to decorate Ramillies could be one of the most important commissions of her career. And it looked as if her career was going to be her whole life from now on.

Her secret dreams of combining it with marriage and motherhood seemed unlikely to be fulfilled. Most of the men she met were already married or divorced. Unrealistically, perhaps, she had always hoped that the man of her dreams wouldn't be encumbered with the debris of a marriage which had gone wrong. He would have had other relationships, that was inevitable. But one of Mark's attractions had been that at thirty-three he was still single, having, like her, concentrated on his career plans.

After her lunch-date, with a friend who was also a busy career woman, Olivia went back to her flat and changed the severely plain suit she had bought in New York, where she found many of her clothes. In its place, she put on a two-piece of dove-grey cashmere, the top having a soft cowl-neck and the skirt hugging her hips and then swirling into folds.

It wasn't the kind of outfit she would normally wear at the office, but she hadn't forgotten Ludovic's caustic gibes about feminism. If his preference was for women who concealed their capabilities behind a screen of overt femininity, then that was how she would handle him.

Now that she was older, and wiser in the ways of the male sex, she realised that, despite his height and physique, somewhere in Ludovic's psyche there were hang-ups which made him unable to accept women on equal terms.

Selecting a moonstone brooch to pin in the folds of the cowl, and matching ear-rings, she acknowledged that she had handled him badly before. She wasn't going to make the same mistakes this time.

'Mr Webb is here, Miss Hartley,' said her secretary's voice, on the intercom.

'Send him up, please, Grace.'

Olivia took a deep breath and rose from behind her desk to open the door to Ludovic as he came up the stairs to her room at the top of the building.

Near the door was a mirror she had designed. In it she caught a brief glimpse of her reflection: swingy, almost shoulder-length hair, large eyes made even larger by dark grey pencil and mascara, a mouth luscious with lipstick and gloss. Invisible, but enhancing the effect she wanted to create, was the expensive French scent she had sprayed on her hair and, lifting her skirt, on her thighs. It had appealed to her sense of humour to use this technique to allure, for professional reasons, the last man in the world she would wish to attract in her private persona.

Pinning on a welcoming smile, she opened the door. 'Mr Webb. . . What admirable timing. You obviously share my passion for punctuality.'

'My schedule depends on it. I expect yours does too.'

As he had on that never-to-be-forgotten morning soon after her nineteenth birthday, he offered his hand.

But this time his smiling appraisal was that of a man who found himself confronted by a woman very much to his taste.

'Very much so,' Olivia agreed. 'Please come in.' She gestured for him to pass her, outwardly calm but inwardly somewhat shaken by her involuntary response to a magnetism she had expected to find less potent now that she was older and more experienced.

Then he had worn casual clothes. Now he was dressed for the city, in a superbly tailored suit of finely striped navy blue worsted with an ivory silk shirt and one of the most beautiful ties she had ever seen on a man. She wondered if it had been picked out for him by a woman—perhaps his wife.

As far as she knew, he hadn't been married before, but perhaps he was now. He was about the same age as Mark, but looked like a man who would want sex more often than Mark, whose libido had been eroded by his liking for rich food and wine.

Nine years had not altered Ludovic Webb's lean build or slackened the taut definition of that formidable jawline. Nor could immaculate tailoring disguise the vigour of his body, any more than the velvet-sleek pile of a jaguar's pelt disguised the deadly power of its musculature.

With a shock, she realised that the man looking appreciatively round her studio-cum-office was in fact far more formidable now than in her memory of him. She wasn't the only one who had matured. He too was subtly altered.

CHAPTER THREE

'SHALL we sit over here?' She gestured towards the comfortable three-seater sofa with its back to the large window overlooking the tiny but charming roof-garden she had had made.

Strategically, sitting at one end of the sofa would be better than facing him from behind her desk. That would give her an authority she didn't wish to assume yet; an authority a man of his sort would subconsciously resent.

'You're much younger than I expected,' he said, waiting for her to seat herself. 'Surprisingly young to have achieved such a high reputation in your field.'

'Perhaps I'm older than you think,' she said, smiling. 'And I've always worked very hard. My work is my life.' As that statement might not please him, she added, 'I hope it won't always be that way. I'd like to enjoy everything life has to offer a woman. But not all those goals are attainable just by hard work. Meanwhile, I find my job very absorbing. But I don't need to explain that to you. From what I've heard about Ramillies, you must feel the same way.'

Ludovic lowered his tall frame into a relaxed position at the other end of the sofa, stretching one long arm along the back of it. His sleeve, with the unbuttoning buttons which were a hallmark of London's finest tailors, revealed the prescribed glimpse of double cuff discreetly linked by small discs of navy enamel rimmed with gold. He did not, as

43

Rathbone had, wear a signet ring engraved with the family crest on his little finger. His nails were well-kept but not professionally manicured like Mark's.

'What have you heard about Ramillies?' he asked, taking in her long slender legs, today encased in opaque dove-grey Lycra to match her dress. Her suede shoes, specially made for her by an up-and-coming young designer, were the colour of black grapes, like the wide belt cinching her waist.

Actually, Olivia had avoided hearing or reading about Ramillies. A couple of years ago, a television programme about the college had been picked out for don't-miss-viewing by the television critic of her pre-ferred national newspaper. She could have watched it, but hadn't. But it had been impossible to avoid all knowledge of what had happened to the house since she last saw it.

'I've met people who've been on the courses you run. They all say what an extraordinary achievement it's been—to transform a decaying mansion into one of the most successful adult arts and crafts schools in the country.'

'It was a struggle at the beginning, but it's up and running now. Enthusiastic word-of-mouth recommen-dations have been the making of us. I expect that's been an important factor in the success of your business.'

'Mine began to take off when a house I had decor-ated was featured in an internationally influential magazine. As a result, I had so many enquiries it was a problem coping with them all. That was before I had set up my present team. We can cope with anything now. . .and be selective about the commissions we take on.'

This had been true at one time, and would be again, but it wasn't at present. They needed this commission. But Olivia knew that nothing succeeded like success. She had to sell him the illusion that clients were lining up for their services.

'You've seen what we did at Hertington Castle. I expect you'd like to look at some other commissions. I've picked out a couple which seemed particularly relevant.'

Two large albums, covered with fabrics she had designed and stamped with her logo, were on the end-table at her elbow. She handed one to him and laid the other on the sofa beside him.

'While you're looking through them, would you care for some coffee or tea, Mr Webb?'

Ludovic glanced at his watch. 'A quarter to six. Is a gin and tonic an option?'

'Certainly. Ice and lemon?'

'Please.'

She felt him eyeing her back view as she went to the small refrigerator behind a panel of the painted cane-work she often used to hide unsightly radiators. All the time she was fixing the drinks, omitting the gin from her own glass, she had the sensation of being watched.

Was it possible that, while they were talking, some-thing about her had rung a bell? If he realised who she was, she hadn't a hope in hell of being selected.

Firmly closing her mind to memories of their first meeting, and the painful year after it—memories which still made her angry—she unscrewed a jar of toasted almonds and shook some into a small bowl.

As she carried one tall glass and the Chinese bowl to his end-table, she saw that he was studying photographs of a house she had done for the warden of an Oxford college.

As she placed them beside him, he looked up. 'Your decorating style seems to lean to the masculine rather than the feminine. But you don't go in for power-dressing I notice.' His glance swept over the curves of her figure as she inclined her body towards the table.

Olivia straightened, annoyed by her involuntary response to that fleeting appraisal. In fairness, it had been too brief to be classed as an undressing look. After all, she had chosen her outfit with the intention of looking as feminine as possible within the bounds of good taste. That being so, she could hardly blame him for registering her breasts and hips. She was similarly aware of the wide shoulders and long, powerful thighs inside his elegant suit.

What she resented was the little stab of excitement she had felt when he looked at her. She didn't want to be attracted to him. It was only because of the pressure of economic events that she was seeing him at all. After what he had done to her grandfather, she had hoped never to set eyes on him again.

Returning to the cupboard for her own glass, she said, 'My aim has always been to crystallise my clients' taste. I've tried not to be a designer whose style is instantly recognisable in every project they do. I don't think that's what first class decorating is about.'

As she returned to the sofa, Ludovic startled her by asking, 'Are you free to have dinner with me?'

As she stared at him, taken aback, he added, 'There's a lot to discuss. I'd like to show you some photographs of Ramillies. But I left them in the car because I wanted to meet you before going into the project too deeply. Already I'm fairly certain that—if we can come to terms financially—you're the right person for the job.'

This was even more disconcerting. Could he really have made up his mind on the basis of twenty minutes' conversation?

'I am free this evening. . .yes,' she agreed.

'Good. May I use your phone to book a table?'

'Of course. Do you know the number you want?'

'It's in my diary.' From an inside pocket of his jacket he produced a small black leather book and, after rising, moved to her desk. He didn't tell her which restaurant he was ringing, or ask if she knew it or might prefer to go elsewhere.

But that shouldn't be a surprise. Everything she knew about him indicated a man who charged through life making decisions to suit himself, with little if any thought for their effect on others. Even the way he tapped the buttons on the keypad of her multi-purpose telephone was a reflection of his character.

She always pressed the buttons with the soft eraser on the end of one of the many pencils she kept in a decorative pot next to the phone. Ludovic jabbed at the keys with the tip of his longest finger, not bothering to check the numbers on the display panel. Olivia always checked. He took it for granted he had dialled correctly. It was another small pointer to the incompatibility of their personalities. She wondered if she would find him impossibly difficult to work with.

'Good evening. This is Ludovic Webb. Is table four free this evening? Excellent. My guest and I will be there in about half an hour. Goodbye.' As he replaced the receiver, his eye was caught by the painting on the wall behind her desk. He checked the artist's signature in the lower left-hand corner.

'I thought so. I also have some of his paintings, including a superb one of Venice. Where is this? Obviously somewhere in South East Asia.'

'It's the flower-market in Bangkok.' She didn't add that she had bought it as a reminder of her backpacking year and her first love.

Returning to the sofa and picking up his gin and tonic, he said, 'You weren't at the private view of his last exhibition in the autumn. Had you been there, I should have seen you.'

Ignoring the implied compliment, she said, 'No, I had another engagement that night. I went to the exhibition the following day, but by then both the paintings I'd have liked to buy had red stickers on them.'

'Which were they? Can you remember?'

'One was a picture of three people having lunch in the shadow of a vine, somewhere in the Mediterranean. The other was a snowscene—a great eighteenth-century urn on a stone plinth in the garden of a country house.'

'I was the buyer of both those pictures. We seem to have similar tastes, Miss Hartley.'

She said lightly, 'He's a very popular artist. He has hundreds of admirers.'

'All the same, it seems a good omen for our association, don't you think?' The teasing gleam in his eyes made her wonder how broadly he defined the word 'association'.

Probably because her attitude to him was predetermined by what had happened in the past, it hadn't occurred to her that he, not knowing they had met before, might fancy her.

At that moment the telephone trilled. It was her

personal assistant, calling from the downstairs office to ask if it was all right for her to go home.

'Yes, Grace. See you tomorrow. Goodnight.'

Olivia had checked her hair and lipstick before Ludovic's arrival. She had only to put on her coat to be ready to leave for wherever he was taking her. She fetched it from the cupboard on the landing: an elegant showercoat of deep violet microfibre which looked like matt silk. It had a soft, light filling, making it very warm. It had cost a lot of money on a trip to Germany last year, but the cut and finish were top-class. It was an investment she would wear through several winters.

As she brought it into the room, Ludovic drained his glass and put out his hands to take the coat from her.

'Thank you.' She turned her back and slipped her arms into the sleeves.

'Does the fact that you haven't rung anyone to say you'll be out for dinner mean you live on your own? Or merely that your partner is also out tonight?' he asked.

'I don't have a partner, Mr Webb. Do you have a family?' she asked.

'No, I'm a bachelor. . .but not a confirmed one,' he added.

His car was parked by a meter a little further along the street. It was as opulent as the one she remembered him driving. As she slid into the passenger seat, and swung her feet on to the deep-pile carpet, she could smell the leather upholstery. When Ludovic, after checking that her coat wouldn't be caught in it, closed the door, it shut with the unmistakable sound of top quality coachwork.

She knew from the registration number that the car

was this year's model. If he could afford to buy new cars of this order, the college must be making substantial profits, and he must be taking a hefty salary out of them. When the time came to talk money, she would drive a hard bargain.

He drove in a manner appropriate to city streets, not in the flashy watch-me style of some owners of powerful cars. She couldn't fault his driving.

At one point it crossed her mind that he might be taking her to the same place Mark had chosen for last night's termination of their partnership. That *would* put her off her stroke.

'Where are we going?' she asked.

'To a private club—the Nabob. Have you been there?'

'No, but I've heard of it.'

What she had heard was that it was very exclusive—as exclusive as the best of London's famous gentlemen's clubs—and consequently extremely expensive.

'I think you'll like it. It's one of the few places in London where, even when every table is occupied, you can still hear yourself speak. The acoustics are excellent and the tables have enough space between them to make private conversation possible. It's popular with people who want to have serious or intimate conversations. The subscription and the size of the membership are designed to stop it going bust without becoming overcrowded.'

'A difficult balance to achieve,' she said drily. 'Are women allowed to be members?'

'Not only allowed. . .encouraged. We have two women on the board of management.' He turned his head to glance at her. 'And, as you do, they both disguise their hard-headed business acumen behind a façade of feminine charm. But everyone knows they have iron fists inside their velvet gloves.'

'You think I have an iron fist?' she asked, smiling.

'I don't underestimate the will-power it's taken you to get where you are. You have to be a lot tougher than you appear, Miss Hartley. Or may I call you Olivia?'

His use of her first name sent a frisson of apprehension through her. Might it remind him he had once met a girl called Olly?

'If you wish.'

His attention was once more on the road ahead and, glancing at his strong profile, she saw he was smiling slightly. Perhaps at the coolness of her assent. He probably wasn't used to being kept at arm's length by women. But if he thought that because she had agreed to dine with him their relationship was going to be personal as well as professional, he was mistaken.

And then, as the car purred to a standstill at traffic lights, and the long lean fingers of its driver shifted the gear-change into neutral, it occurred to her that if he did have that in mind it would be a very satisfying retaliation for what he had done to her grandfather to seem to be an easy conquest.

And then, when he thought he had her where he wanted her, to give him the biggest set-down of his all-conquering life.

The Nabob Club had American-style valet parking. Ludovic handed over his keys and a young man in smart dark blue and gold livery took charge of the car while they went into the club.

'Good evening, madam. Good evening, Mr Webb.'

The hall porter had a blue and gold striped waistcoat
under his cutaway coat.

Before Ludovic signed the book, he said to Olivia,
'You can leave your coat with Connie. Her domain is
the first on the left down the corridor.'

As she went to the ladies' room, Olivia saw that, as
its name suggested, the club's décor was inspired by
the time when men from Europe had made huge
fortunes in the Orient, particularly in India, returning
to the West to be known as nabobs. It had been
Rathbone Webb who, years ago, had told her the word
was an anglicisation of the Urdu word *nawwab* meaning governor or powerful landowner.

Even in the cloakroom the chairs were embedded
with pieces of iridescent shell and the walls hung with
paintings of Indian palaces.

Ludovic was chatting to another member when she
emerged, but he quickly excused himself and came to
join her, taking her lightly by the elbow and steering
her into the waiting lift.

'The dining-room is on the top floor, with a rather
nice view of the river,' he told her.

As the lift carried them upwards, Olivia looked
closely at an aquatint of the Red Fort at Agra. But, as
she studied it, she was intensely aware of the man
beside her, his height and muscular build emphasised
by the confined space in the small lift.

All her life she had disliked the feeling of being shut
in. Had she been a member here, she would have used
the stairs rather than risk being in the lift by herself
during a power failure. It was her only neurosis and
she supposed it derived from some forgotten experience in early childhood.

But, as she stepped out of the lift into an ante-room

leading to a bar on the left and a dining-room on the right, she realised that for once she had not experienced her usual sense of claustrophobia. It had been overridden by the powerful physical magnetism of the man with her. She also knew that, if the lift had stopped and they had had to wait for some time before being released, she wouldn't have had to fight down irrational panic. Much as she disliked and distrusted him, she was forced to admit that Ludovic was the sort of person who, in any kind of emergency or tight corner, could be relied on to know what to do.

'Would you like another drink before we dine?' he asked, with a gesture at the bar.

'I don't think so, thank you. . .unless you would. But if you're driving back to Ramillies, I expect you're watching your intake.'

'That's no reason why you should restrict yours. However, if one is your limit, we'll go straight in.' Again, he put his hand under her elbow.

The ritual of courteous greeting was repeated by the restaurant manager, who conducted them to their window table, screened from its neighbours by banks of exotic plants. A fat candle was already alight inside a storm glass, its soft light adding to the sheen of the silver, crystal and starched damask on the table.

The fleshpots of London, New York and several other world capitals were no novelty to Olivia. Many times, both as guest and host, she had eaten in places like this. Yet tonight she was reminded of her first experiences of the world of rich, elegant living, before she had gained the confidence to feel wholly at ease.

Tonight she was on the *qui vive* again. Not because she would have any problems understanding the menu or knowing the correct way to eat some unfamiliar

dish her host might urge her to try, but solely because
of the man who had brought her here. Although she
knew some things about him, to a great extent he was
an unknown quantity, and one she wasn't totally sure
she could handle.

'I expect you eat out a lot,' he said, when the head
waiter had left them to study the menu, presented in a
folder illustrated with more aquatints of India's famous
buildings.

'Why do you say that?'

'An attractive unattached woman isn't likely to have
many blanks in her diary.'

'In my observation, people whose work is important
to them keep quite a strict rein on their social activities. Do you dine out a great deal?'

'I don't live in London. Most of the time I'm at
Ramillies, where I eat with our students in the refectory. They're an interesting crowd, particularly some
of the mature students. Last night my neighbours at
table were a retired Concorde pilot, who had come to
learn to throw pots, and a clergyman's widow who, in
her seventies, decided to take up glass-engraving.'

'Oh, you've forgotten to bring your folder of photographs of the college,' said Olivia.

'I didn't forget. I'd be interested to see how you've
decorated your own living quarters. I'm hoping you'll
invite me back to your place for coffee and we can
look at the photos there,' he said blandly.

His audacity took her breath away. Did he also have
it in mind to make a pass at her? The thought of how
he might go about it made her insides churn. She had
no doubt he would make love with the same masterful
assurance which seemed his approach to everything.
But not to her. Never to her! She might allow him to

kiss her, although not tonight, but only to intensify the impact of her subsequent rebuff.

She said coolly, 'I'm afraid that won't be possible. My living-room is out of commission. It's being redecorated.'

'What about your kitchen?' he suggested.

Speaking the truth this time, she said, 'It's a one-person galley—there's nowhere to sit. Why not ask for your folder to be fetched? The car can't be far away.'

'Very well. I'll do that. . . After we've made our decisions.' He gave his attention to the menu.

Had he believed her excuse? Olivia wondered, as she scanned the list of dishes. If she played hard to get, would it sharpen his appetite for conquest?

In keeping with the club's ambience, there were various Indian dishes on the menu, but she decided to start with a Caesar salad, followed by fish cakes with parsley sauce. There might be women on the board, but the menu included a lot of traditional men's club food, she noticed. After the fish cakes, she would try the chef's apricot ice-cream.

'You make up your mind very quickly,' Ludovic remarked, as she closed the menu.

'I usually do.'

'What are you having for your main course?'

'The fish cakes.'

'Snap,' he said, his eyes glinting. 'And what would you like to drink with them?'

She had assumed he would choose the wine, although here the list was included with the menu not, as in many restaurants, offered separately and not usually to women, unless they had made it clear they would be paying the bill.

Olivia's knowledge of wine had been inculcated by an elderly antiques dealer who had become a friend.

'I see they have a 1990 Meursault. Have you tried it? Do you like it?' she asked.

'An excellent choice. That's what we'll have.' With a slight nod of the head he brought the head waiter to his side.

As Ludovic talked to him, she watched the way the candlelight accentuated the characteristic Webb nose and chin. There were now a few silver threads in the thick dark hair at his temples, which had not been there nine years ago. In other respects he looked younger than many of his contemporaries. She wondered how he kept fit. There was still a toughness about him which set him apart from men like Mark and Alistair Hamilton. Even if they belonged to health clubs—which Mark needed to, but didn't—they didn't have Ludovic's air of ruggedness. They were civilised men. He, she suspected, was not. There was a streak of the savage in him.

As the head waiter finished making notes, she turned to look out of the window at the view of the Thames.

'And I wonder if you would ask someone to bring up a cardboard file I left in the back of my car,' she heard Ludovic say, adding his registration number.

'Certainly, sir.'

For a few moments after the waiter had gone Ludovic didn't speak, and she knew he was studying her as, minutes earlier, she had studied him.

'Tell me how and where you started your career?' he said, after the pause.

'I won a competition jointly sponsored by one of the glossies and a school of interior decoration. The prize was a six-month crash-course at the school, after which someone I knew in America used their influence to get me taken on as a gofer by a famous New York decorator. When I came back to London, the same person put up some money for me to set up on my own.'

'Was that person a man?'

'A woman. A friend of my family,' she added. It was true in the sense that, when small, she had regarded Rathbone in much the same light as her real grandfather.

'Where does your family live?'

'They're all dead now.'

'Mine too. I don't remember my mother. She drowned when I was three. Her life-line snapped after she'd been washed overboard in a storm in the Roaring Forties.'

Olivia's instinctive reaction was a surge of compassion for anyone left without a mother at so young an age. She herself had been seven when her parents' accident had left her in the care of George Jones, her mother's father. She could remember being cuddled and kissed by her mother, while Ludovic could have no memories of the woman who had borne him. Olivia could also empathise with the last frantic thoughts in *her* mind as she found herself adrift in a raging ocean.

'Did your father remarry?' she asked.

'No, they had mated for life, as a few lucky people still do. Sometimes, when I was older, there were women who shared his cabin for short spells. But there was no question of marriage. He'd been married once and that was it. But, of course, my mother was an exceptional woman to have gone with him in the first place. Even then, there weren't many girls who thought the world well-lost for love. They're an extinct species now.'

'I wouldn't say that,' she countered. 'The sort of men who inspire those feelings aren't too thick on the ground, you know.'

'Would you give up your career for a man?'

'Probably not, but then I see it as a vocation rather than a career. I know it's not in the same category as medicine or nursing, but to me it's more than merely a way of making money.'

At this point three of the staff converged on their table: the waiter bringing their first courses, the wine waiter, and a junior porter bringing Ludovic's file.

When they were alone again, she asked, 'Was sailing your father's profession or his pastime?'

'It was his way of life. He'd crewed for the boat's original owner and then had her left to him. He didn't have enough money to be described as a yachtsman—barely enough to keep her seaworthy at times—but sailing was the only thing he could do. So he scratched a living chartering, or carrying what freight we had room for.'

Ludovic paused to bite off a piece of the toast on which he had been spreading pâté.

'My schooling was paid for by Dad's English uncle. Dad had promised my mother he'd see me decently educated, even if it meant going cap in hand to his rich relation in the UK. He hated having to grovel and he made sure I spent the holidays with him and didn't get too big for my boots. I never met the old man from whom I inherited Ramillies.'

'Why was your father hostile towards his English relation?'

'Because they'd disowned *his* father. With good

reason, I shouldn't wonder. But, whatever the truth of that was, Dad grew up with a deeply ingrained resentment of inherited power and privilege. He regarded himself as a man of the people and detested all top dogs. Any airs and graces I brought back from my expensive boarding-school were very quickly squashed.'

Olivia knew there was only one school in England to which Rathbone would have sent his unknown heir: his own Alma Mater, Eton. She couldn't help thinking it must have been a strange existence for an adolescent boy—half of it spent at a bastion of the Establishment, and the other half crewing for an anti-Establishment father.

'Did you know you would inherit Ramillies?'

He shook his head. 'I thought there were others ahead of me, so to speak. Dad encouraged that belief. So it was a surprise to find myself, at twenty-seven, the owner of a crumbling mansion. No money went with it because, in the last of several quixotic gestures, my predecessor had given what was left of his funds to help children who had lost limbs in the war in Afghanistan. I couldn't quarrel with that. They needed help more than I did. I already had my life mapped out.'

'Doing what?' Olivia asked, deeply curious to know about his life between leaving Eton and arriving at Ramillies. At the same time she knew she was treading on thin ice, because talking of those times might remind him of the last of Ramillies retainers, whom he had sent packing, and for whose ignominious death he must be held partly responsible.

'I had a finger in several pies—a charter company in the Caribbean, a group of small-boat flotillas in the

Greek Islands and a small publishing firm specialising in charts and sailing guides. All that was much more in my line than a run-down estate. My first thought was to sell it.'

'What changed your mind?' she asked.

He picked up the glass of wine he had already tasted and drank some more, his expression abstracted. Then his mind returned from wherever it had travelled and his mouth took on a sardonic twist. 'As with most of life's major decisions. . .*cherchez la femme.*'

Her heart gave a nervous lurch. 'A woman changed your mind?'

Ludovic replaced his glass. 'But that was in another country and—to misquote—the wench is married. She and I were heading in that direction, but we didn't make it.' He leaned towards her, looking into her eyes. 'How about the men in your past? Anyone serious?'

His gaze was strangely mesmeric. She found it hard to look away. 'No,' she said, spearing the last of her salad with her fork. It was none of his business anyway. She was still shaken by the shock his '*cherchez la femme*' had given her, making her think, for a second or two, that he had been referring to herself.

'Too busy career-building, hmm?'

'As your sex has always done. Men never hang about waiting for Miss Right to show up. They get on with their lives. That's what women do now. . .have for a long time. Who gave you the idea of turning Ramillies into a college?'

'Again, *cherchez la femme.*' He paused while their main course was served, the fish cakes accompanied by a platter of colourful vegetables.

'I met an elderly lady who had been to a summer

school held at a university during the vacation,' he
went on. 'She'd enjoyed the workshops, but she hadn't
liked the accommodation in the students' residences,
and the food had been dull and institutional. She gave
me my blueprint.'

'Mmm. . .these are delicious,' said Olivia, enjoying
her first taste of the perfectly browned fish cakes which
had seafood as well as fish in them. 'There must have
been a lot of problems before you could implement
the blueprint, mustn't there?'

'Innumerable problems,' he said drily. 'But I like a
challenge.'

Something in the way he looked at her as he said it
made Olivia wonder if that was his attitude to women:
a series of challenges to his masculinity.

CHAPTER FOUR

'IF YOUR predecessor had given his resources to war relief, what did you use for money?' asked Olivia.

'Fortunately it was a time when a lot of venture capitalists were looking for projects to invest in. I managed to raise the funds I needed without losing control. How are you placed? Do you have full control of your business?'

Olivia nodded. 'But mine is very small-scale compared with the size and scope of your operation. I have only five employees. . .plus a much larger team of outworkers who aren't actually on my payroll. You must have a very large staff.'

'Not as large as you might suppose. Most of our tutors are freelances who are only at Ramillies two or three times a year, depending on the popularity of the classes they run.'

It wasn't until the meal was over and the table cleared of everything but coffee-cups and wine-glasses that Ludovic retrieved the folder from the window-ledge and turned it so that its contents would be the right way up for her.

Olivia prepared to mask any emotions which might be aroused by photographs of her old home.

Ludovic opened the folder. 'This is the south front of the house.'

For the next few minutes, with pauses to drink his coffee, he showed her the house as it was now, much changed from the way she remembered it but also poignantly familiar.

At one point he suddenly broke off an explanation of recent extensions to say, 'You have the most beautiful eyelashes. . .not spoilt by all that gunge most women put on them.'

She gave him a startled glance. 'Thank you.'

He smiled at her, in no hurry to resume the matter in hand. She wondered if he knew enough about women to guess that she didn't need mascara because her eyelashes were dyed at the salon where she had her hair cut.

Her manner deliberately brisk, she brought his attention back to the ground plan on the page in front of her. 'What is that block used for?'

By the time they left the club, it had been arranged that she should go to Ramillies the following Saturday, staying overnight and returning to London the next day.

'You could stay over till Monday, if you like?' he suggested, as they waited for the lift. 'It would give you more time to get the feel of the place.'

'It would also mean enduring the Monday-morning traffic-crawl as all the weekenders return. I'd rather avoid that by coming back late on Sunday.'

'As you wish. But I think when you've seen what we have to offer, you'll find it quite hard to tear yourself away. Most people seem to feel that way.'

Olivia's apartment was in a block built at the beginning of the century, with the spacious proportions and high-quality woodwork of the period. The block was managed by a tenants' association which had recently voted to step up security by paying for twenty-four-hour porter service. After ten o'clock at night the main door was secured, so that even residents had to ring for admission. Usually the night porter came out of his little office immediately he was summoned and could be seen through the small glass panes in the upper part of the main doors. But tonight he didn't appear.

Olivia had explained the system to Ludovic as he escorted her from the car to her doorstep.

'Please don't wait. I'm sure he won't be long, and you have a long way to go,' she said.

'It's a very easy run at night when the roads are quiet. I shall play a new tape I bought today. Do you like music, Olivia?'

'I often play tapes when I'm working. Certain music helps me to concentrate. Here he comes now.' This as she spotted the porter emerging from the lift. 'Goodnight.' She held out her hand. 'Thank you for a good dinner and an interesting evening.'

'I enjoyed it too.' Ludovic retained a firm hold on her hand until the porter opened the door and apologised for keeping her waiting.

She tried to withdraw her fingers from Ludovic's but found she couldn't. Then he lifted her hand and brushed his lips on her knuckles. 'Until Saturday. Goodnight, Olivia.' With a friendly nod at the porter, he walked back to his car.

'I'm glad you had the gentleman with you, Miss Hartley. It's not nice for a lady to be alone in the street after dark these days. I was upstairs with Mrs Standish. Her bathroom light needed a new bulb and she couldn't get the glass shade off.'

Sometimes Olivia spent five or ten minutes chatting. Tonight she had too much on her mind.

With a smiling goodnight, she made for the staircase.

* * *

On Saturday morning she set out for Ramillies with an overnight case on the back seat of her small car. For an ordinary weekend in the country she would have worn jeans, with her chamois-coloured needlecord shirt and the navy gilet which at the moment lay on the seat beside her.

But jeans might be the key which unlocked that 'not-wanted-on-voyage' section of Ludovic's memory to which an annoying young girl called Olly had been relegated nine years ago. For that reason she was wearing a skirt of soft country tweed, its hem and pockets bound with leather, and chestnut-brown tassel loafers with thick soles, suitable for walking.

As she left London behind, Olivia wondered which bedroom she had been allocated and whether Ludovic had been sincere in saying she seemed the right person for the job.

It was certainly true—although he didn't know it— that no other contender would have her intimate knowledge of the house and its history, her feeling for what designers called the *genius loci*, meaning the special atmosphere of a building and its environs.

She wondered why old Mr Webb had never mentioned the boy who was his unknown heir. Perhaps because even to think about him reanimated the pain of losing his own son, whose photograph and decoration for gallantry had been on the table by his chair all the time she had lived at Ramillies.

Today, as on the day she had dined with Ludovic, the cameo ring bequeathed to her by Rathbone was missing from her little finger. The carving was not a human head, like the majority of cameos, but the profile of a hawk—part of the Webb family crest. During Rathbone's lifetime, the ring had been among the many mementoes and curios he kept in a special cabinet. Why he should have left it to her was something she had never been able to fathom.

Not that it was of any great value, except by association. The bezel framing the cameo and the ring were of pinchbeck, not gold, and the stone itself was slightly chipped. For her it had great sentimental value and she wore it every day. But she couldn't wear it in front of Ludovic. It would give the game away instantly. He would be sure to recognise the hawk and want to know how she had come by it. She could tell him she had bought it. Family heirlooms often came on the market. There was even a shop in London specialising in crested china and silver once the property of landed families. But she didn't wish to lie to Ludovic, if she could avoid it. Even the subterfuge of pretending to be on her first visit to Ramillies bothered her. Then she thought of the five people depending on her to pay their salaries, and of her grandfather, driven to drink by Ludovic's betrayal of his great-uncle's trust, and her qualms subsided.

Halfway there, before leaving the motorway, she stopped for petrol and coffee at a service area. As she was leaving, a car like Mark's was arriving. But for Ludovic's sudden incursion into her life, she would have given more thought to Mark's decision to stop seeing her.

He had been right in saying she had never been enthused by the prospect of becoming a politician's wife. The obligation to be polite to Mark's constituents, the arbitrary disruption of their private and social life if the party whips required his presence in the debating chamber or when a vote was being taken, and much else about his career had made her reluctant to take the final step towards regularising their relationship.

Mark had proposed several times, and each time she had put him off. Maybe, ten years from now, when she was still on her own, she would regret it.

Once she had left the motorway and was nearing her destination, thoughts of Mark and of her future were driven from her mind by the excitement of returning to Ramillies.

As she approached the main entrance, her eyes widened at the sight of the gateway restored to its orginal splendour and the lodge beside it looking equally spruce. The gates were standing open, but a few yards inside was a barrier.

When Olivia touched her horn, a man in a peaked cap emerged from the lodge.

'Is it Miss Hartley?'

She smiled and nodded. 'Good morning.'

'Good morning, miss. You'll see the signs to the car park. It's not far from the house, but if you can't manage your luggage, the girls in the office will send someone to carry it in for you.' As he stepped back, he gave an informal salute.

Olivia would have driven slowly anyway, taking in all the changes to what she could see of the grounds. But, in addition to being tarmacked, the drive now had rows of traffic bumps to prevent anyone speeding along the mile-long approach to the house.

The car park was surrounded and divided into bays by shrubberies which would prevent the rows of vehicles from spoiling the view from the house. Olivia was locking her car when Ludovic's voice said, 'Good morning,' and she turned to find him striding towards her.

Like her, he was wearing a gilet over a shirt, but his was dark green, enhancing the military air given by his soldierly bearing.

'The gate-keeper let us know you had arrived. Welcome to Ramillies.' He held out his hand.

'Thank you. What a lovely morning.'

'Spring's in the air. Is this all your luggage?'

'I always try to travel as lightly as possible. I hope what I've brought for tonight won't be too informal.'

'I should have warned you if you'd needed to dress up. I thought you might like to eat with the new intake of students,' he said, picking up her case. 'From time to time I do use the dining-room, for private dinner parties, but this weekend it's in use for a business conference.'

It wasn't until they left the car park that she had her first full view of the familiar façade in its new guise. In her time it had been smothered with ivy, encroaching even over the windows. This had now gone, revealing the rose-coloured brickwork mellowed by long exposure before the ivy took over. In its place other creepers had been planted, but were not being allowed to mar the symmetry of the windows, their panes shining in the sun, their woodwork immaculate white instead of flaking grey.

'Like it?' Ludovic asked, looking down at her.

'It's beautiful.' It had always been that, to her, but she had to admit it was far more beautiful now.

'All the best bedrooms are occupied by the conference people. We want them to be impressed and recommend us to other organisations. I should have liked to give you one of the south front rooms, but I'm afraid you're at the back.'

'I'm sure I'll be very comfortable wherever you've put me.'

They entered the building by way of the pillared porch built to shelter guests arriving in their carriages, and the changes made to the interior were even more startling.

Accustomed to shabby, sun-frayed curtains, their rails and rings heavily cobwebbed, and thick dust on every horizontal surface from the broad ledges of the cavernous stone fireplace to the narrow ledges of the oak panelling, she could not at once adjust to the hall as it was now.

Dust still danced in the beams of sunlight slanting through the tall windows, but none veiled the beautiful patina of the furniture and the panelling. The curtains had been replaced and, cleaned and repaired, the oriental rugs formed a pathway of rich dark colour across the well-swept stone floor.

As she was taking it all in, a woman appeared at the far end of the hall.

'There's a telephone call for you, Ludovic.'

He turned to Olivia. 'Would you excuse me? Annette will show you your room. I'll bring your case up as soon as I'm off the phone.'

Taking it with him, he disappeared into what had been the gun-room.

The woman came to shake hands. 'I'm Annette Trent, Ludovic's secretary.' She looked about fifty and emanated efficiency.

'Have you been at Ramillies long?' Olivia asked, as they walked towards the Grand Staircase, now immeasurably grander with its new carpet and the tapestries cladding its walls cleaned and repaired.

'Since soon after Ludovic took over. What a sad

state it was in then! The previous owner was very old and eccentric. He and a decrepit old manservant lived here all on their own. Imagine a house like this with only two people in it.'

Inwardly, Olivia was bristling. Presumably Mrs Trent—she was wearing wedding- and engagement-rings—had received the impression of decrepitude from Ludovic.

'It must have been like a tomb then,' the older woman continued, as they mounted the wide shallow stairs at a leisurely pace. 'Even now, when it's full of students, it never seems crowded. Actually, the new intake of seven-day students and the conference people don't arrive till this afternoon. So you'll have the house more or less to yourself until they start filtering in about tea-time.'

Although Olivia had not forgotten the original lay-out of the house, she quickly became confused by the fresh paint, additional fire doors and structural altera-tions to the former servants' quarters.

'We've put you in number fifty-four, which used to be one of the linen-rooms,' said Mrs Trent. 'It's small, but it has its own bathroom and a view of the kitchen garden.'

A few moments later she opened the door of a room with a brass-railed single bed, its apricot cotton cover matching the floral chintz blind and dress curtains.

'This is delightful,' said Olivia. 'As this room faces north, this warm colour is just what it needs to make it cheerful. I recognise this design. It's an early Jane Churchill, isn't it?'

Mrs Trent nodded. 'I chose it. I've used a lot of her materials in my own house because they're so pretty and inexpensive. At the beginning, Ludovic asked me to help him with the redecoration, but then it got to the point where we needed professional help. The first decorator we had was very good, but he was extremely expensive, and Ludovic felt that he was using Ramillies as a place to show off his more flamboyant ideas, some of which worked, but not all. This house has a strong personality of its own.'

'I'm sure it has,' Olivia said, warming to her.

At this point Ludovic appeared and put her case on a luggage stand next to the large Edwardian wardrobe.

'Do you think, after you've unpacked, you'll be able to find your way back to the hall?' he asked. 'There is a fire escape diagram on the back of the door, which shows that it isn't the labyrinth it seems to be on arrival.'

'I may take a few wrong turns, but I'm sure I'll soon get my bearings.'

'In that case, as soon as you're ready come down to Annette's office, next to the bottom of the main staircase, and I'll collect you from there. We'll start with a walk round the grounds. As we're dining with the students tonight, I'd thought we'd have lunch *à deux* in my private quarters. See you in about half an hour.'

His secretary was already in the corridor when Ludovic left the bedroom and turned to close the door. The last look he gave Olivia before he disappeared from view was not the polite smile of a prospective employer for someone whose only appeal lay in her professional skills.

The glint in his dark blue eyes was definitely that of a man looking at a woman in whom he had a far more intimate interest. Reading his mind, she knew that what he would like to be doing was closing the door from the inside and spending the interval until lunch-time on the bed with her.

'Mrs Trent looks immensely capable,' said Olivia, as they were beginning their walk.

'She's invaluable,' Ludovic agreed. 'Her husband died two years before I came here. He was only forty. She was left fairly comfortably off, but she needed something to do, both her children being at boarding-schools. She had good secretarial skills but had been turned down for several jobs because she couldn't use a computer. That wasn't a drawback here as we had no computers to begin with. Now she and I are both competent at the keyboard, but not as clued-up as her younger son, who's a genius with anything electronic.'

'Does she live in the village?'

'They moved here a couple of years before she was widowed. The house was large, in line with their plan to have a second batch of children. Then Andrew was found to have a terminal illness. Three years ago, when the boys went to college, I offered her one of the staff cottages. She now lives on the estate, with a spare room for her sons when they're on holiday. But mostly they're doing vacation jobs or travelling. She wants them to feel free and this way they do. . .more so than if she were on her own in their old house.'

'You'd think by now she'd have married again,' said Olivia. 'She comes over as a very nice person.'

'She's a sweetie,' he agreed. 'But, from all I've heard, Andrew Trent was also a great guy. After twenty years with him, she's not going to settle for second-best.'

'From what you told me the other night, most of the

people who come here are out of the ordinary. They must include unattached men.'

'Maybe. We don't enquire into people's marital status. We get a fair number of married couples, often taking different courses and not seeing much of each other except at night in their rooms. I hope you're not unhappy with the size of your room.'

'Not in the least. I like it. . .and Mrs Trent's choice of décor. I couldn't have done it more attractively myself.'

'We're bidden to lunch at her cottage tomorrow. Annette has her meals in the refectory most of the time, but she likes to cook once a week. She's made the cottage very nice. The house she had before had an equally relaxing atmosphere. She's a born home-maker, with all the diverse skills that underrated *métier* demands.'

His remarks reminded Olivia of the cook he had borrowed from friends when he was first at Ramillies. She had liked Mrs Oakes. It was on the tip of her tongue to ask after her, but she recognised the *faux pas* just in time.

Ludovic misinterpreted her silence. 'I expect your generation regards making jam and doing patchwork as an anachronistic waste of time,' he remarked.

'Not so: I don't make jam because I almost never eat it, but I never fly without a piece of needlepoint in my hand luggage and I enjoy doing flowers.'

'I'll introduce you to our head gardener and get him to organise a basket for you to take back tomorrow. He also has a staff cottage and rarely takes any time off. We'll probably find him in the greenhouse.'

The vast Victorian greenhouse had lost most of its glass and become very dilapidated the last time Olivia had seen it. Now it had been restored to its former splendour and was the source of the beautiful pot plants and ferns she had noticed all over the house.

After talking to the head gardener, they completed the circuit of the house before returning indoors to Ludovic's quarters on the sunny south-west corner of the first floor.

Showing her into his sitting-room, he said, 'This is one of the rooms I'd like you to redesign. It has always been used as a bedroom, but I sleep in the room next door, with the adjoining dressing-room converted into a bathroom. As you can see, I've hidden most of the rather unattractive wallpaper with pictures. Going round the house, at the beginning, I came across all these paintings of sailing ships which I've grouped together. Before, they were dotted about all over the place.'

'I expect there were wonderful things in unexpected places, weren't there? There usually are in old family houses. Did you take expert advice?'

'Yes, Bonaby's came down and gave the place a thorough going-over. What can I get you to drink?'

'Have you any Campari?'

He nodded. 'What d'you like with it? Soda?'

She saw there were slimline tonics on the drinks tray. 'With tonic and ice, please. May I look round?'

'Of course.'

'You were saying that Bonaby's came down,' she prompted, moving away to scan the crowded bookshelves.

Mark had never had time for reading. He had watched all the political programmes on TV and skimmed a wide range of newspapers and magazines, but books were not part of his life as they were of hers and, it seemed, of Ludovic's. The books in this room were new. They had not been in the house when she'd lived there.

'They did a complete valuation and the sale was very successful. Without it, I couldn't have begun to put the place in order.'

'Didn't you mind selling things that belonged here? Apart from the ones Bonaby's thought too far gone,' she said, thinking of the tapestries on the Grand Staircase.

'When it came to the point, I didn't sell as much as Bonaby's would have liked me to. I had second thoughts,' he said, bringing her drink to where she was surveying the pieces he had assembled for his personal use. 'They were rather annoyed when I changed my mind about selling up lock, stock and barrel. They still made a handsome commission on the stuff which was auctioned. Junk, most of it. But the sale took place at a time when people had money to burn and made crazy bids for anything with a provenance they could boast about. An old lavatory seat with a crack in it would have fetched a good price if it had come from a lordly loo.'

The remark reminded Olivia of his crack about her lavatory brush hairstyle.

'I'm going to have a beer. If you think your kitchen is small, come and see mine.' He beckoned her to a door leading into a small ante-room between the bedroom he had converted and another bedroom beyond.

'In a house this size, it's a long trek to the kitchen for a late-night sandwich. With a microwave, a fridge and this small sink I don't have to risk an encounter with the Ramillies ghost,' he said, smiling.

As she had a little while earlier, she only just managed to stop herself saying, Ramillies hasn't any ghosts.

Instead, she said lightly, 'I'm sure any ghost who saw you coming in the small hours would smartly dematerialise.'

'Do I make *you* nervous, Olivia?' His blue eyes were suddenly intent.

'What a strange question. Of course not.'

She would have turned away to go back into the sitting-room, but he put a hand on her wrist.

'Yet sometimes you give the impression of being. . . not entirely relaxed.'

She had brought her Campari with her and, without risking spilling it, could not escape his light clasp.

'You're imagining it.'

'Perhaps. . . Or perhaps you have other reasons for being a little on edge.'

'I'm not aware of being on edge,' she said untruthfully.

If his fingers had been nearer her pulse, he would have had conclusive proof that she was extremely edgy. Normally her pulse-rate was sixty. Now, because he was touching her, it had revved up to eighty or more.

'But I am aware,' she went on, 'that, even staying overnight, I'll still have my work cut out to assimilate all I need to give you some storyboards and rough estimates.'

Ludovic released her wrist. 'I assumed it might take several weekends for you to absorb the atmosphere and work out some ideas. This isn't a rush job. If we see eye to eye, it could extend over years.'

'Do you mind if I ask you who else you've approached?'

'At this stage, no one. If I were employing a builder, I'd get several quotations. Engaging a designer is different. Hertington Castle is proof that you know what you're doing. Unless your ideas and estimates are way out of line with mine, I expect this to be the beginning of a long and close association.'

He said this with a look which set her pulse racing again. There was no mistaking the double meaning. She would have had to be unusually naïve not to recognise the underlying message. He wanted her. It had been in his eyes when he closed the door of her room. It was there again now, a clear signal demanding an answering signal. Yes or no. Come on or back off.

Choosing her words with some care, she said, 'I hope so too. But it's early days yet. As you say, everything depends on whether we see eye to eye about the character of the house and how best to reflect it.' Moving into the sitting-room, speaking over her shoulder, she went on, 'So you didn't have to sell any of the nicer things?'

'A few, but none of the pieces I particularly liked. Now, with the help of a retired archivist, I'm going through the family papers and writing a history of the house with notes on the finest paintings and pieces of furniture.'

'I would have expected your upbringing to make you an outdoor person, not interested in history and books. But obviously you are,' she said, with a gesture at the bookshelves.

'I wasn't much interested in the past until I came here. But a house like this is so steeped in history that it makes everyone interested.'

Remarks like this were beginning to show him in a new light. Olivia was conscious that, had they not met before, she would have been warming towards him intellectually as well as being dangerously attracted to him.

At that moment someone knocked at the door and, after Ludovic went to open it, a girl in a white overall with her hair in a white cotton snood pushed a trolley across the threshold.

He introduced them. 'This is Carol, one of our kitchen staff. Miss Hartley is a famous interior designer.'

Later, when Carol had laid the table and departed, Olivia said, 'I think "famous" was an overstatement. To be famous today, you have to appear on television.'

Ludovic drew out a chair and waited for her to sit down. 'Why don't you appear on television? I should think you're very photogenic, and there must be a large female audience for programmes which tell them how to improve their houses.' He moved to the opposite chair. 'Or do you prefer to keep your trade secrets to yourself?'

'I should love to do a programme like that, but I don't have an entrée to the world of television and there are many designers far more famous than I. Top-level interior design is like *haute couture* and *haute cuisine*—still dominated by men. There've always been a few exceptions. But if a TV producer wanted to set up a series of that kind, I doubt if he'd think of me.'

'That's a refreshingly honest answer,' he said. 'I can think of people who, to swing a contract their way, would pretend to have producers beating a path to their door. Are you always so open, Olivia?'

For an unnerving moment she wondered if the

question was edged with mockery; if he had recognised her and knew that, far from being open, she was being extremely devious.

'I hope so. . .most of the time,' she said uncomfortably.

Ludovic said, 'We all have to tell white lies sometimes. I often think it would make life a lot more interesting to speak the unvarnished truth, the way very young children do before they're trained to equivocate.'

They took the lids off their soup bowls, releasing a fragrant aroma of vegetables and herbs.

It was a simple meal: the soup followed by a Spanish omelette and salad, and then by cheese and fruit. Their conversation flowed easily. It seemed that, for the time being, he had decided not to follow up that meaning remark in the ante-room.

After lunch, he showed her the dining-room and drawing-room, later to be used by the businessmen.

It was the strangest feeling to walk into rooms where, in her time, the shutters had always been closed and the furniture and paintings hidden by dust-covers. She had known what was under the covers because she had looked, but she had never seen either room lit by daylight or without the covers.

As Ludovic talked about their contents, she could see that his response to them went deeper than mere pride of ownership. But, whatever he felt for the house now, it could never excuse his heartless behaviour in the past and its distressing consequences for Granpa and herself.

CHAPTER FIVE

For the evening meal in the refectory, Olivia changed her needlecord shirt for one of dark bronze silk with a scarf worn like a loosely-knotted tie, and ear-rings which looked like dull gold but were actually a bargain spotted in a Paris street market.

By now the course students had arrived and unpacked and would be converging on the Empire Room for pre-dinner drinks. Like the modern kitchens and refectory, this large purpose-built room took its name from mementoes of Britain's imperial past, in which long-dead Webbs had been closely involved.

The room had been empty when Ludovic had shown it to her earlier, but when she paused on the threshold at a quarter to seven most of the comfortable sofas and chairs were occupied, as were the stools at the bar, where two stewards were busy serving drinks.

As there was no sign of Ludovic, Olivia went to the bar. She was standing behind two men, waiting her turn to be served, when one of them glanced over his shoulder and, seeing her, turned sideways to make a space between him and his neighbour.

'Good evening. It's always a bit of a scrum the first night, when everyone comes in to supper at the same time. Tomorrow they'll be more spaced out,' he said, with a smile.

'You've been here before, I gather,' she said, smiling back. He was a few inches taller and a few years older than herself, with friendly hazel eyes and light brown hair.

'I'm one of the tutors. You don't happen to be one of my students, do you? Picture Framing.'

As Olivia shook her head, the other man moved away and she stepped into his place.

'That's a pity,' said the man who had spoken to her. 'I like teaching pretty ladies.' He offered his hand. 'I'm Ben Frost.'

'Olivia Hartley. How do you and your students make contact?'

'After they've eaten, they find their way to my workshop and I give them an introductory pep-talk. Which course are you on?'

'I'm not. I'm here on business. Have you taught here for long?'

'This is my second course. The first was last autumn. The previous tutor retired and Ludovic Webb offered me the job. I have a small art gallery and framing business near here. What's your line?'

'I'm in interior design.'

'I would have guessed fashion,' he told her. 'I noticed you when you came in. People are like pictures, you know. A postcard can look great with the right mount and frame. A fine painting can be spoiled by the wrong presentation. Most people don't know how to present themselves to the best advantage. You do.'

'Thank you. Who looks after your gallery while you're at Ramillies?'

'My sister. We share the house adjoining the gallery. She's my twin. We both set out to be artists and Hattie spends most of her time illustrating cookery articles in women's magazines and newspapers. I soon realised I wasn't going to make a living with my paintbrush and, being a pragmatic type, settled for a related occupation. What would you like to drink?'

This after the barman had asked, 'What's yours, sir?'

Olivia said to him, 'A slimline tonic with ice, please.'

Ben Frost ordered a beer and insisted on paying for both drinks. 'What brings you to Ramillies?' he asked. 'Are classes in interior design being added to the curriculum?'

'Not as far as I know. I'm here to tender for some redecoration work on the house.'

As she spoke, a small grey-haired woman came up to them. 'Are you Mr Frost?'

'Yes, ma'am.'

She introduced herself as one of his pupils.

The three of them were talking when Ludovic appeared in the doorway, casting an eye over the rest of the room before turning to the bar, where Olivia raised her hand to catch his eye.

'Sorry I'm late. I was held up by a telephone call,' he said, as he joined her.

'It doesn't matter. I've been making friends. Mrs Wright, this is Mr Webb, the owner of Ramillies. Mrs Wright is on Mr Frost's course,' she added.

Ludovic made friendly enquiries about the little woman's journey and whether she found her room to her liking. But, after five minutes of pleasantries, during which the barman brought him a gin and tonic, he said, 'Would you excuse us?' and steered Olivia towards a sofa which had just been vacated by people going to the refectory.

'Tonight the bar will be busy until it closes,' he said. 'But tomorrow, and for the rest of the time they're here, a lot of people will go back to the workshops after dinner. They're here to learn and they don't want to waste a minute.'

'Ben Frost was telling me that his sister is a successful illustrator. Have you met her?'

He nodded. 'A nice girl and very talented, but unfortunately confined to a wheelchair since an accident. It hasn't affected her career, only her private life. She was engaged to be married. Her fiancé broke if off. He's been widely condemned for it. What's your reaction to that scenario?'

'I think it's too facile a judgement to write him off as a rat,' Olivia said thoughtfully. 'I'd give him some credit for knowing that he couldn't cope with the new situation and having the moral courage to face the inevitable odium. In the long run his desertion could be less painful for her than if he'd gone through with the marriage under the duress of public opinion. What do you think?'

'I knew him. They weren't well-suited. He's the athletic type, with no intellectual resources. In my view he did the right thing. With luck, there'll be someone better for her.'

When they joined the diners in the refectory, Olivia found that the self-service counters catered to every taste. She made her choice from the bowls containing a dozen different salads and topped her selection with a couple of rollmops. While she was helping herself to a wholemeal roll from the baskets of bread baked on the premises, she saw Ludovic having a word with the chef in charge of the hot food counter.

He joined her a few moments later and they went to an empty table at the far end of the room where they were soon joined by others. The man who politely asked permission before sitting down next to Olivia

turned out to be a retired professor who was learning
to paint, while the woman who plonked herself next to
Ludovic, and promptly began to relate to everyone
within earshot the problems encountered on her journey to Ramillies, had come for the poetry-writing
course.

Conversation was general, and Olivia was amused
to notice how skilfully Ludovic managed to prevent his
garrulous neighbour from turning it into a monologue.

After dinner he took her on a tour of the workshops
and showed her the shop where students could buy
materials and specialist tools.

Through all this, his manner was much the same as
if she had been a visitor of his own sex. But, after
locking the shop, which was only open when classes
were in progress, he turned to her and said, 'Shall we
have some more coffee?'

Instinct told her that, if she agreed, she would find
herself being escorted back to his private quarters, not
to the Empire Room.

'If you don't mind I'd like to go to my room and
make notes while they're fresh in my mind. As the
bedroom has an electric kettle, and even a teapot, I'll
have a cup of tea while I'm writing. Are all the
bedrooms equipped with the makings for hot drinks?'

'Yes. We try to combine all the comforts of a good
hotel with the feeling of being a guest in a private
house. Are you sure you want to disappear as early as
this?'

'I am here on a working assignment, not a social
visit,' she reminded him.

'All right. I won't lead you astray.' Again, the
message in his eyes was at variance with what he was
saying. 'I'll see you as far as the main stairs, then

check that the conference people have found everything to their satisfaction.'

Once they were out of earshot of the buzz of conversation in the Empire Room, the house was astonishingly quiet for a building housing several hundred people. On the way to the Grand Staircase they saw no one else, and it was easy to imagine they were the only people in the whole vast edifice.

'What time would you like to have breakfast?' Ludovic asked, in an appropriately low voice. 'On Sunday, it's served from eight to nine.'

'At eight, if that suits you.'

He nodded. 'Goodnight, Olivia. I hope you sleep well.'

'Thank you. Goodnight.'

As he went towards the heavy double doors of the drawing-room, further along the wide corridor, she lingered by the massive newel post, half regretting her decision to avoid being alone with him.

Two hours later, with her violet raincoat over ivory silk pyjamas, Olivia flitted silently down the staircase, on her way to the library.

It had proved impossible to sleep. She had finished the one book she had brought with her. But to borrow another wasn't her only purpose. She wanted to see the room which had always been her favourite, although her last memories of it had not been happy ones.

Long ago, in the time when the house had been empty except for the two old men, she had never found it scary at night. Nor did she now. By moonlight it seemed more familiar, more like the place she remembered.

When she opened the library door, the evocative scent of thousands of books still permeated the air. The room was in darkness because the shutters were closed. She felt for the light switch connected to two standard lamps behind two high-backed chairs on either side of the fireplace.

To her delight the chairs were still there. Better still, they had not been re-upholstered with shiny new leather. The old leather had been revived with a special dressing.

Olivia had so many old friends on the bookshelves that it was hard to decide which one to borrow. Access to the highest shelves was by a movable wooden stairway with a platform at the top. She was perched on this platform, browsing through an illustrated book of fairy-tales and legends, when the door opened and Ludovic came in.

His eye drawn to the pools of light by the fireplace, it was a few seconds before he saw her. In those moments Olivia registered that he wasn't wearing pyjamas, only a dark blue bathrobe of Turkish towelling tied with a cord at his waist.

'Oh. . .it's you,' he said, catching sight of her. 'What are you doing up at this hour?' As he asked, he was crossing the room, his soft-soled leather slippers making little sound on the polished boards between the rugs.

'I wasn't sleepy and ran out of reading.'

From the foot of the ladder, Ludovic looked up at her, his hands in the pockets of his robe. 'I couldn't sleep either. I wonder if we were restless for the same reason?'

Olivia was suddenly sharply conscious of being naked but for the thin silk of her pyjamas. The weather was mild at the moment and, although the central heating was off at this time of night, the library had never been as cold as other parts of the house. She had discarded her raincoat before ascending the ladder. It was on the back of a chair some distance from the ladder.

'You don't want to admit it, do you?' Ludovic said, showing his white teeth.

'Admit what?'

'That you were restless for the same reason as I was.'

'I don't know why you couldn't sleep.'

'Yes, you do. Women know instinctively when a man's attracted to them, even if he tries not to show it. . .which I haven't. You knew the night we had dinner together. That's why you wouldn't ask me back for coffee. You were afraid I'd rush my fences. I wasn't planning to. I know it's not your style to go to bed on the first date. If it were, I wouldn't be interested.'

Olivia's throat felt as if it were closing. Disturbing sensations she didn't want to recognise were starting.

'Aren't you rushing your fences now? It's only a few days since we met.'

His removed his hands from his pockets and took hold of the sides of the step on a level with his chest. 'Tomorrow isn't always another day. Hattie Frost took tomorrow for granted and woke up in a hospital bed with her back broken. That could happen to any of us. I'm not saying——' his eyes were amused '—"Be mine tonight, Olivia". I'm just putting my cards on the table, so that you know it's what I shall be saying at the apposite moment.'

She swallowed to clear the tightness in her throat.

'Unless I make it clear that it would be. . . unacceptable?'

'Yes, unless you do that.'

But, for reasons she couldn't explain to herself, she couldn't do that—and he knew it.

'Don't you think it's usually a mistake to complicate working relationships with personal ones?'

'Very often, yes. Not in this case.'

'Why not in this case?'

'We're both free agents. We've been around long enough to know who we are and what we want out of life.'

Olivia closed the book on her lap and replaced it on the top shelf. 'I know that if I don't get some sleep I'm not going to sparkle tomorrow. May I come down, please?'

To her relief he let go of the ladder and stepped back. She didn't even have to descend it with his eyes on her. He must have noticed her coat, and he moved away to fetch it for her.

When he turned round, she was standing at the foot of the ladder, her hands fingering the collar of her pyjama jacket to conceal her breasts. She didn't want him to know that he had succeeded in arousing reactions which were going to make it even harder to sleep now than before.

Ludovic opened the coat and she turned to slip her arms into the sleeves and pull it round her. But no sooner had she done that than she found herself whirled to face him, both his arms firmly round her.

'You don't seriously think I'm going to let you escape without even kissing you, do you?'

For a few seconds more he held her, letting her feel his strength, the impossibility of breaking free even if she'd wanted to. Which she didn't. In those moments her mind surrendered control to her body, and her body responded with atavistic delight to the feeling of being overwhelmed by a superior force

When he kissed her, she responded. She couldn't help herself. His lips persuaded and hers consented.

'I think you'd better hurry back to bed before I forget my good intentions.' Ludovic's voice sounded husky as he raised his head and put her gently away from him. 'Off you go. I'll see to the lights.'

At half-past seven the next morning, Olivia stood under the shower and, closing her eyes, felt again the strong arms, the warm mouth and, moments before he had released her, the unmistakable evidence that, although he had let her go, it hadn't been what he wanted to do.

Or what she had wanted him to do.

It had not been until she was back in her room that she'd come to her senses, remembering who he was, what he had done to someone she loved.

Yet now, as the warm downpour streamed over her naked body, she was aroused again. She wanted him, wanted him madly, in a way she had never wanted Mark.

She went down to breakfast in the shirt she had worn the day before but with different ear-rings. But for the risk that it might cause him to recognise her before she was ready to reveal herself, she would have put up her hair and worn the shirt with its collar up.

Ludovic was reading one of the Sunday newspapers from a selection laid out on a centre table when she entered the Empire Room. Absorbed in a report, he didn't notice her standing in the doorway.

She wondered how long it had taken him to get to sleep. Her knowledge of men was more limited than that of some of her contemporaries, but, from what she knew of male physiology, it wouldn't take much to re-arouse him. Men were programmed by Nature to follow through. If Ludovic wanted her, he wouldn't be discouraged easily.

'Good morning,' she said, in her most businesslike tone. 'Any world-shaking news?' After meeting his eyes for a moment, she dropped her gaze to the array of front pages.

'Good morning. Not really,' he answered. 'How did you sleep?'

'Very well, thank you.'

'Liar,' he said, in an undertone. When she looked up, his eyes were mocking. Keeping his voice down, he went on, 'It doesn't show in your face, but I wouldn't mind betting you lay awake as long as I did.'

Olivia said coolly, 'If it pleases you to think so.'

He folded the paper and replaced it on the table. Moving round to where she was standing, ostensibly scanning the headlines on the tabloids, he said, 'It doesn't please me. I'd rather we had said our good mornings in private and were having breakfast upstairs. Perhaps the next time you come. Meanwhile. . .shall we go in?'

'Do you think this sort of behaviour is in keeping with your position?' Olivia asked, trying to sound more flippant than she felt, as they went to the refectory.

'If you wanted me to think you cold and strait-laced, Miss Hartley, you shouldn't have melted in my arms so moreishly last night,' he murmured in her ear.

Olivia could think of no answer that he wouldn't

counter with another provocative statement. She decided silence was the best way to deal with him.

The display of breakfast foods was as appealing as the selection last night. She helped herself to muesli, a carton of natural yogurt, wholemeal toast and some honey on the comb.

Ludovic was still loading his tray with a more substantial breakfast when she collected cutlery and a paper napkin and carried her tray to a table where four of the eight chairs were already occupied. No conversation was in progress, but she quickly got one going with an enquiry about the others' courses. She waited for Ludovic to join them before she started her breakfast, confident that he wouldn't be able to bait her in the presence of four strangers, with two more to come.

She had underestimated him. The table had its full complement, and Ludovic had been making himself pleasant to the last comer, a man with a nervous habit of clearing his throat between every few words, when suddenly he looked at her and said blandly, 'When you were in the library last night——'

As he paused, she had a vivid memory of being held fast in his arms with his mouth about to come down in that spine-tingling kiss. As if she were in her late teens instead of rapidly approaching the end of her twenties, she felt herself starting to colour up.

'Did you notice the board blocking off the empty hearth?' he continued.

She had, and had been amused by the realistic effect. 'I thought it was very cleverly painted.'

'It was done by Hattie Frost. She used to sell chimneyboards before she began to concentrate on cookery illustration.'

Olivia knew he had mentioned the board only to remind her of last night. Speaking to the woman on his left, she said, 'Mr Webb is referring to a painting of four cats washing themselves. Are you a cat-lover? I prefer dogs myself.'

'Oh, I *love* cats,' his neighbour enthused. 'But I hadn't realised you were the owner of Ramillies.' As Olivia had surmised she might, given the right cue, she began to ingratiate herself.

She was still talking his ear off when, a few minutes later, Olivia finished her breakfast and rose, 'Would you excuse me?' she said, to the table in general.

The other men remained seated but Ludovic half rose from his chair. He was still eating toast and marmalade and would have to put up with the sycophantic gushing on his left for some time yet.

After leaving him to it, she returned to her room to brush her teeth and collect her things she would need for her morning's work: her camera, a sketchbook and an expanding steel rule. There being no architect's plans to copy and work from—or none that she knew of—at a later stage she would have to send down her assistants to take all the necessary measurements. For the moment, photographs and sketch-notes were all she needed to work up some ideas to present to him. Even with the changes which had been made, her intimate knowledge of the house was a huge advantage.

When she went downstairs, she half expected Ludovic to be lying in wait for her, bent on revenging himself for being set up for the effusions of the woman in the too-tight pink jumper.

But it was Ben Frost who was sitting on a chest near the foot of the staircase.

'Good morning,' he said, getting up. 'When I couldn't see you in the refectory, I thought it wouldn't be long before you came down.'

'Good morning. I've already been down once and had breakfast.'

'One of the early-birds, were you? I had mine at home. As I'm local, I don't live in like the other tutors. I told my sister about you. She was very excited. You're her favourite interior designer. I hadn't made the connection, but the way her bedroom is done up is copied from a photograph of a room you designed.'

'Really? I wonder which one?'

'Could you find time to come and meet her? It's on your way back to London, not a major detour. It would be a big thrill for Hattie. . . And I'd like it too,' he added. 'I shan't be there this week, but you'll be coming down regularly, I imagine?'

'That depends on whether my ideas find favour.'

'There's not much doubt about that. According to Hattie, you're brilliant.'

Olivia smiled. 'I'd like to meet your sister. If you give me your address, and if it's convenient for her, I could stop off for half an hour on my way back later today.'

From his billfold Ben produced a business card with a thumbnail sketch of the Old Barn Gallery in one corner.

'Hattie's at home most of the time. Two years ago she was smashed up in an accident. It's left her unable to walk and not too happy about driving. Her car's been adapted. She could drive. But it's hard to get back her nerve.'

'I'm sure it is,' Olivia said sympathetically. 'What a

good thing you run a gallery. It must make her feel less isolated than she would be without it, doesn't it?'

'Yes, it keeps her in contact with people outside our immediate circle. Some of her friends—people she thought were friends—have backed off since she was crippled. She was going around with a sporty, fun-loving crowd, because she was in love with a guy who was heavily into water-skiing and autocross. He was one of the defectors. She's probably better off without him, but it was hard to take, on top of everything else. But she's over that and working hard at her career. She has a lot of grit, my sister.'

Olivia was warmed by the pride and affection in his voice.

'Having you to keep an eye on her must be a big plus. I always longed for a brother. As a matter of fact, I invented one. It was lonely, being an only child——' She stopped short, swallowing the words 'in a big house like this'.

'That's not unusual, I believe. What did you call your imaginary brother?' Ben asked.

Ludovic came round the corner, raising an eyebrow when he saw them.

'I think you'll find most of your group ready and waiting for the off, Ben,' he said, his tone somewhat crisp.

The tutor looked at his watch. 'We're not due to start until nine-thirty.'

'They won't object to starting early, and Miss Hartley has a lot to do.'

The implicit dismissal triggered a clear recollection of the way he had once dealt with Olivia. 'Now please leave the house. And don't come back.'

When Ben had excused himself and was out of

earshot, she said, 'Do you find that arbitrary manner is accepted by your staff? My people wouldn't like it.'

'Ben needs keeping in line. He's good at teaching, not so good at time-keeping. Was he chatting you up?'

'No, telling me about his sister. What time do we need to leave for lunch with Mrs Trent?'

'Twelve-thirty.' He had noticed the things she was holding. 'You'll need help with the measuring, won't you?'

'Not this morning. I only need to concentrate. I work better on my own,' she added pointedly.

'Don't worry: I have no intention of distracting you. I also have things to do. Coffee or tea and biscuits are served in the refectory at eleven. I may see you there. In the meantime, if you want to have another look round my private quarters, please do. I shan't disturb you. I'll be out of doors.'

By mid-morning Olivia had used three rolls of film and her sketchbook was full of drawn and written notes. She still hadn't adjusted to the strangeness of being back in the house she had always regarded as home until Ludovic came and dispossessed them.

Perhaps it wasn't fair to think of what had happened in those terms. Ramillies had never been theirs, and it wouldn't be the way it was now if he hadn't come and applied his energy and inspiration to pulling it back from the brink of decay.

But the good things he had done for Ramillies did not and could never atone for the terrible effect of his treatment of her grandfather. That ought to be on his conscience forever; except that a man with a conscience would never have acted as he had.

At eleven, instead of going to the refectory, she

went to her room to make coffee. Finding the door open and one of the maids busy there, she then went outside to sit in the sun on a secluded bench she had noticed the day before. Deliberately, she had not been near the room which had once been her bedroom. The past was over and done with; nothing would be served by recalling those idyllic years of childhood. She hadn't really grown up until she came back.

'Annette cooks lunch for a dozen people on alternate Sundays,' Ludovic told her, on the way to Mrs Trent's cottage. 'Usually there are two couples from among those she knew when her husband was alive, and the rest are people on their own who might otherwise get left out of the social whirl.'

'That can't apply to you,' said Olivia. 'Unattached men are always in demand socially. As owner of Ramillies, I should have thought you'd be liable to too much lionisation.'

'I did get a lot of invitations in the first years I was here. My great-uncle having been a recluse, people were curious to see what I was like and what state the house was in. Now it's no longer a mystery, I'm less in demand,' he said drily.

But she guessed it was by his own wish if he went out less than before. Tall, personable and unmarried, he would be a desirable addition to any hostess's table.

She had already noticed that some of the trees she remembered had disappeared, and concluded that they must have been victims of the hurricane-force gales which twice in the last decade had destroyed fine old trees all over southern England. She asked Ludovic how much the estate had suffered, and he was still explaining the new forestry methods he had introduced when they reached Mrs Trent's home.

That Ludovic was a frequent visitor was indicated by the fact that, instead of ringing the bell, he opened the front door and signed for Olivia to enter, at the same time raising his voice to call, 'Are we the first comers, Anny?'

'Yes. . . I'm in the kitchen,' came the answer.

Wearing a striped butcher's apron, Mrs Trent was at the sink, rinsing the remains of a purée from the bowl of a food processor.

'I'm a bit behindhand this morning. Hello, Miss Hartley. Ludo, I'm relying on you to buttle for me, as usual.'

'Of course. These are some chocs to go with the coffee.' He put the package he was carrying on the worktop before turning to ask what Olivia would like to drink.

Bearing in mind that she would be driving later, Olivia asked for wine.

'Red, white or pink?'

'White, please.'

He opened the door of the large fridge, where several bottles of wine were standing in a compartment inside the door. Annette was opening the package.

'Ooh. . . How extravagant! You must have got these in London. I shall pass them round once and keep the rest as cook's perks,' she said, with a wink at Olivia.

Her manner was subtly different from when they had met yesterday. Clearly it was her nature to be outgoing and friendly with everyone, but today she was even more relaxed. Perhaps because there was a wine-glass with half an inch of wine left in it near the

hob. Or perhaps for another reason. When a good-
looking man gave a lonely woman expensive hand-
made chocolates, the gesture was liable to seem more
meaningful than the donor intended, thought Olivia.

CHAPTER SIX

LUDOVIC had dealt with the drinks for Annette before. He knew where she kept the corkscrew and opened another drawer for the stoppers with which he replaced the drawn corks.

'Don't throw those away,' said Annette. 'I give them to Ben for his framing students.' She turned to Olivia. 'If a painting has to be hung on a wall which might give off damp, small slices of cork attached to the back of the frame allow air to circulate. But perhaps you already knew that tip?'

'I did, actually. I know a very good framer in London and he told me about it. I met Ben in the bar last night, and later today I'm going to call on his sister,' she added. 'Apparently, her bedroom is a copy of an illustration of a room I did for someone. Do you know Hattie?'

Annette nodded. 'Most people round here know each other. It's one of the nice things about living in the country. Have you always lived in London?'

'Not always.' Olivia hoped she wasn't going to be asked where she had lived before. Although her work had taken her all over the country, there was no area she knew well enough to claim as hers.

However, at this point there was a loud rap on the front door and Annette excused herself to go and welcome some more guests.

'Cosy, isn't it?' said Ludovic, glancing round the large room with its collection of baskets arranged along the top of the wall cupboards and the large, scrubbed deal table laid for lunch with brown earthenware side-plates, gingham napkins and half a dozen small clay flowerpots overflowing with the plant called mind-your-own business as table decorations.

'Yes, very,' she agreed. 'And whatever is in the oven smells delicious.'

'Some sort of casserole, I expect. Annette cooks for outdoor appetites and leaves the pretentious stuff to the upwardly mobile.'

'Whom you, from the top of the local social pile, regard with contempt,' said Olivia, surprising herself.

She supposed she ought to be flattered that he hadn't recognised her as one of the upwardly mobile. But she wasn't. His remark had flicked her on a raw spot. She wasn't normally sensitive about her origins. Why should she be? The world of Rathbone Webb's day, with its rigid divisions between rich and poor and the layers between those extremes, was long-gone. In the present meritocracy, being the granddaughter of a butler was something to proclaim, not to hide—except in these particular circumstances.

In the act of taking some more white wine out of the fridge, Ludovic paused to give her his raised-eyebrow look.

'What prompted that verbal slash?'

'I'm sorry. Perhaps I sounded sharper than I meant to,' she conceded. 'But I've done a lot of work for the so-called upwardly mobile, and disparaging jokes about them annoy me. Centuries ago, your forebears were upwardly mobile. Ramillies was built by the new rich of their day. In any century, those are the people who make a country prosperous. By striving to better themselves, they improve everyone's lot.'

'Provided they don't lose sight of——' He broke off as Annette brought in the new arrivals and began introducing them.

When all the guests had arrived, and Annette had announced that lunch was ready if they would take their places at the table, Olivia found herself at the opposite end from Ludovic. He was on Annette's left, with an older man on her right. Olivia was between the husband of the woman she had been talking to before lunch and a boy of about nineteen, who had not yet outgrown a bad case of teenage acne and looked very ill at ease.

Olivia's own teens were not so far behind her that she had forgotten the pain of being fat and awkward. She determined to put him at ease and soon discovered that, like their hostess's younger son, this boy, Guy, was a computer fanatic.

Although Olivia's knowledge was limited to the programs used in running her business, she knew enough to ask intelligent questions about the applications and games he was using on the powerful system he had built himself.

It wasn't until Annette called down the table to ask him to help clear the plates on which she had served a delicious lamb and lentil casserole that Olivia had an opportunity to chat to her other neighbour.

'You're a stranger in these parts, Olivia,' he said, having read her name on the slip of paper tucked between the tines of her dessert fork. 'As you can see, I'm Tim, and I work for the Forestry Commission and live in Lynchet Parva next to Andy and Anny's old house.'

Olivia explained her presence and then asked, 'Have you lived in the village long?'

'About fifteen years. We were here in old Mr Webb's time, but of course no one ever met him. He wasn't the friendly fellow that his successor is,' he said, with a glance along the table to Ludovic's place.

But Ludovic was not there. Glancing over her shoulder, Olivia saw him opening some more bottles of wine while Guy rinsed the dirty dishes before loading them in the dishwasher and Annette attended to the next course she had prepared for them.

While Olivia was looking at them, Annette broke off what she was doing to put her hand lightly on Ludovic's arm and murmur something in his ear, something which made him grin and exchange a conspiratorial glance with her.

Returning her attention to Tim, Olivia said, 'Did you never run into the people who ran the house for him?'

'There were only two. . . A cleaning woman and a rather surly manservant. I saw him in the village shop sometimes, but never had any conversation with him. Nor did anyone. He kept himself to himself. Died of DTs about a year after old Webb, so we heard. Butlers are all reputed to hit the bottle, aren't they? I should think living in that house, before it was brightened up and modernised, would be enough to drive anyone to drink.'

It took all her self-control not to say angrily, That wasn't what drove him to drink. It was being cheated by the charmer you all think so highly of, being bundled into an institution, which finished him.

But she couldn't set the story straight now and, because she needed the long-term work Ramillies offered, might never be able to do so. The defamatory tales would continue to circulate, and there was nothing she could do about it.

There was a choice of pudding: a large treacle tart, its glistening golden filling latticed with twisted strips of pastry, and individual coffee meringues, filled with a nutty cream mixture. Most of the men chose the tart, while the women—protesting at the calories they contained—opted for the meringues.

'I can see you don't have to worry about calories,' said Tim. 'Or cholesterol,' he added, regretfully passing on a bowl of whipped cream without helping himself.

'Does that mean you're a desk-forester rather than an actual woodman?' she asked.

''Fraid so. Wish I were more active. Mowing the lawn is my most strenuous exercise.'

While cups of coffee were being handed round in one direction, Ludovic's box of chocolates was circulating in the other. Biting into a black chocolate with an elegant squiggle of milk chocolate on the top and a melting mouthful of raspberry fondant inside, Olivia remembered the intimate exchange she had happened to see a little while earlier.

Was the out-of-office-hours relationship between Ludovic and Annette merely friendship? Or was there more to it than that? Although some years his senior, Annette was an attractive woman, and some men liked a fuller figure, as long as it was reasonably firm and the proportions were right.

The possibility that, by coming on strong with her, Ludovic might be cheating his present mistress made Olivia very angry indeed.

Of course, she didn't know for certain that *was* the situation, but it shouldn't be too hard to find out.

However discreet people were, in a rural society such as this it was almost impossible to conceal an affair. Someone would have seen something gossip-worthy and the word would have spread. As Annette was very likeable, many people might be hoping the liaison would end happily for her, even though her biological clock was perilously close to midnight and the chance of her giving Ludovic an heir was a slim one. But it might be that as Ramillies was no longer a private house he wasn't bothered about having a son to follow him.

By half-past three there was no sign of anyone leaving. There had been some changing of places, but no glancing at watches, or other signals that it was time to go home. It looked as if the party might continue until half-past four or five, when Annette would probably make tea and produce a home-made cake.

Olivia had already packed her case and checked out of her room. At a quarter to four she rose and approached her hostess.

'That was a marvellous meal, Mrs Trent. Thank you so much for including me. I've enjoyed it enormously, but I must tear myself away and get back to London. There's no need for you to disturb yourself,' she added, as Ludovic, who had been speaking to his other neighbour, concluded the conversation and rose to his feet.

'I also have things to do. Thank you, Annette. You put on a great Sunday lunch. It will take about four circuits of the park to work off what I've eaten, but it was worth it.'

He had placed his hand on her shoulder and gave it

an affectionate squeeze before lifting it in a wave to the others at the table.

'Do you really run round the park?' Olivia enquired when they were outside. 'Or was that a figure of speech?'

'People who don't exercise become couch potatoes, like Tim. Running isn't my favourite thing—when there's time, I'd rather go rock-climbing—but, however busy the day, there's always a space in the schedule for a half-hour run. What were you and that lad with the spots discussing through the starter and main course?'

When Olivia told him, he said, 'Judging by the look he gave you as we were leaving, he's seriously smitten. I doubt if he gets that kind of attention—any attention—from girls in his age-group.'

'Probably not. Most teenage girls judge boys by their looks, and Guy's face is a bit of a mess at the moment. But if you ever have problems with Ramillies's computer network, I'm sure he could sort it out as fast as an engineer. . .and he didn't have to be told how to load the dishwasher. He's also a Wendy Cope fan, another point in his favour. She's a very funny and shrewd modern poet, but Guy's the first male I've met who's read her poetry.'

'It sounds as if you have a lot in common,' Ludovic said sardonically. 'It'll be interesting to see if he has the enterprise to pursue this meeting of like minds.'

'Don't be absurd,' said Olivia. 'When I was his age, someone of mine seemed on the brink of middle-age.'

But, as she spoke, she knew it was partly because she had been attracted to Ludovic when he was in his late twenties that what he had done had been so peculiarly painful, leaving her, all these years later, still burdened with unexpressed rage.

'On the contrary, callow youths are traditionally drawn to older women. . .and sex is said to be a great cure for acne.'

It crossed her mind that perhaps he was speaking from experience. She couldn't imagine him ever being plagued by spots. His taut olive skin had probably always been smooth, even during adolescence. But his first experience of sex might well have been with someone older.

Irritated by seeing in her mind's eye visions of the young Ludovic being taught to make love by someone similar to Annette, she said, 'That's an out-of-date myth, and Guy has too much intelligence to see himself as some all-conquering stud.'

'Your vehemence suggests you've had trouble with that species.'

It had been, and perhaps he knew it, an oblique dig at him, provoked by the things he had said before breakfast; his assumption that, because she had returned his kiss in the library last night, they would soon be having an affair.

'I've always tried to avoid them, but some of my girlfriends have had problems.' Regretting being rattled, she added, 'It was a very good party, wasn't it? I wonder how late the other people will stay?'

'The later the better, from Annette's point of view. Unless her sons are at home, the evenings are lonely for her. Because she entertains, she gets asked out a good deal, but, at the end of the day, there's always that empty room at the top of the stairs.'

She wondered how he would react if she said what was on her mind: Have you ever slept in that room?

They had reached the house, where Olivia had left her case under a heavy oak table.

'What about next weekend?' he said, on the way to the car park. 'We can give you a nicer room.'

'Thank you, but I shan't need to come again until you've seen and approved some roughs. If they're satisfactory, we'll move on to the costing stage. I've a very busy week ahead. It may be a fortnight before I can send you my proposals.'

'Come on a private visit. . .just to unwind,' he suggested, as she unlocked the car and opened the rear door so that he could put her case inside. 'Come on Friday and have two nights here. You're a bundle of tensions, Olivia. I was watching you during lunch. You were listening to Guy and Tim, giving them all your attention, but there was something on your mind. . . Something which expresses itself in various small nervous mannerisms I don't think you're even aware of.'

'You must have been watching me very closely.'

'I was. There's something about you. . .' He paused, looking into her eyes with a faint frown contracting his eyebrows.

For a moment she felt a strong impulse to declare herself, to have it out with him, get it over.

Then he threw her by bending down to kiss her lightly on the mouth. 'Drive carefully. I'll be in touch.'

She could still feel his lips on hers when the gatekeeper raised the barrier for her. With an effort she put Ludovic out of her mind, to concentrate on her driving and the route to the Frosts' art gallery.

An 'OPEN' notice was displayed at the entrance and there were two cars in the parking area. Sunday, if the weather was fine and townspeople went for a run in the country, was likely to be busier than weekdays, thought Olivia, as she cast a professionally critical eye over the exterior of the converted barn.

If she hadn't been forewarned, she might not have noticed immediately that the girl behind the reception desk was sitting in a wheelchair. Hattie Frost's long-lashed brown eyes and her lively expression were what caught the attention first.

'Are you Miss Hartley?' she asked eagerly.

Olivia smiled and nodded. 'And you're the creator of those amusing cats in the library at Ramillies.'

Hattie beamed. 'Did you like them? I used to sell a lot of chimneyboards, but it's an exhausted market. Cookery features are booming. I'm working on food for next Christmas. Would you like to have a look round? As soon as these people have gone, I'll close up and make you some tea. It's a great thrill to meet you.'

'What time does your brother get back?' Olivia asked, later, when she had been shown the bedroom copied from pictures of her work and they were in the Frosts' sitting-room-cum-studio.

'About nine. He has dinner with his group, and then if they want to work late he stays on, although not usually until the workshops close at ten. Have you seen Ben today?'

'Very briefly, this morning. I was invited to lunch by Mrs Trent. Do you know everyone at Ramillies?'

'Ludovic has been coming to private views at the gallery for a long time. Sometimes he drops in to see me out of the blue. I like him, but he makes me nervous,' Hattie confessed, with a sheepish laugh. 'He doesn't intend to, he just does. He's seen so much more of the world than Ben and I have, and he has a way of making poker-faced jokes that I don't realise *are* jokes until I see that smiling look in his eyes.'

'I know what you mean,' said Olivia.

'Do you?' Hattie said doubtfully. 'You don't look as if anything would faze you.'

'Only because I've learnt not to show it. . .or not very often. Do you know Mrs Trent?'

Hattie nodded. 'Ludovic introduced us. When she's baking, bottling, or whatever, Annette gives me a call and Ben takes me over to draw or paint in her kitchen. I'll show you.' She wheeled herself to a storage unit, coming back with a sketchbook which she gave to her guest.

Turning the pages, Olivia found a series of pen and wash drawings recording the activities in Annette's kitchen during the year.

While she was admiring them, Hattie said, 'I've also done sketches of the kitchens at Ramillies and the vegetable garden. The head gardener is very kind. He gives Ben veggies to bring home for me to paint— Savoy cabbages, artichokes and bunches of grapes from the hot-house.'

'What happens to your drawings after they've been used as illustrations?' asked Olivia. 'Do you sell them in the gallery?'

'When I put some in the rack where we keep a selection of unframed paintings, they didn't go.'

'I think they're delightful—the ideal wall decorations for a vegetarian restaurant I'm decorating. I'd like to buy a dozen, if Ben will mount and frame them in the way I want.'

'That's no problem.' Hattie's dark eyes glowed with pleasure. 'I'll show you the whole lot.'

While Olivia was making her selection from a crowded portfolio, she brought the conversation back to the lunch party. She felt bad about pumping Hattie, but she couldn't resist indulging her curiosity by asking, 'Are Ludovic and Annette more than friends, d'you think?'

'There's a lot of gossip about them, but nobody knows for certain,' said Hattie. 'Annette was very happily married, and she's a bit prim in some ways. But maybe that's just on the surface.' She paused. 'I think Ludovic could overcome anyone's reservations if he exerted himself. One of his previous girlfriends was an artist who taught at Ramillies for a couple of years when the college first opened. After she left he had something going with a woman who runs a riding-stable. But that was a few years ago. He may have someone in London. He goes there a lot.'

Olivia stayed for two hours, giving Hattie a cheque for the paintings she had selected and arranging to bring them back when she had decided on the size and style of the frames.

As she continued her journey, she felt ashamed of herself for taking advantage of Hattie's lack of discretion. The girl's loneliness made her more of a chatterbox than if she had plenty of companionship. It hadn't been fair to make use of that tendency.

If you wanted to know, you should have asked him point-blank, Olivia told herself crossly.

She got home to find a parcel waiting for her. It contained various items of hers that Mark had found in his flat: a cotton robe and travel slippers, a shower cap, toothbrush and paste, hand-cream, two paperbacks and various pens and pencils.

In the accompanying note, he asked her to return anything of his she came across. As a postscript, he added that if at any time she needed his help, she had only to call him.

Reflecting on the two relationships which constituted her 'past', Olivia wondered if her life would have been happier if she had done what her first love, Tom, had wanted, and gone back to New Zealand with him.

She had loved him, and had hurt for a long time after their parting, and she had hoped to love Mark. But it hadn't happened. There had never been any magic in their relationship. It had grown out of a mutual need for a partner at social events, someone to share holidays, someone to go to bed with. It had worked pretty well in the first two categories, but in bed they had never been attuned, and that side of things had deteriorated.

Until this weekend she had never been sure whether this had been because Mark was an unimaginative lover, or because she was undersexed. Now she was certain she wasn't. Ludovic's kiss in the library had set her alight the moment his mouth closed on hers. Instinct told her that in his arms all kinds of wanton responses, never aroused by Mark, would well up and overwhelm her.

But did she want that side of her nature brought to life, and especially by a man she could never love or even respect? She had already recognised the impracticality of her original intention to encourage him in order to rebuff him.

As a woman journalist had written recently, hell *did* have a fury greater than a woman scorned. It had the fury of the dominant sex when they found they couldn't kiss the girls and make them cry any more, or were on the receiving end of their own time-honoured tactics.

If she made a fool of Ludovic, she could wave goodbye to a lucrative and long-term connection with Ramillies. She wasn't in a position to do that.

The following Thursday evening, Olivia was at her drawing-table when the telephone rang. Some intuition told her that the caller was Ludovic.

But it wasn't his voice she heard after she said, 'Hello?'

It was the night porter. 'There's a Mr Webb to see you, Miss Hartley.'

Regretting that she hadn't had the answering-machine on, which would have allowed her to pretend to be out, she said, 'Send him up, would you, Maurice?'

In the few moments' grace before he reached the first floor, she flew to her bedroom to scramble out of her jeans and sweatshirt and into a pair of fine wool trousers with a matching midnight-blue sweater. There was barely time to comb her hair and dash on some lipstick before the bell rang.

'Good evening.' Ludovic smiled at her. 'I hope I'm not interrupting anything.'

'I'm working this evening, but as you're here. . .' She stood back for him to enter.

Evidently it was raining outside. The shoulders of his pale raincoat were damp.

'I've had a dull day in the corridors of power. I called in the hope that you'll have dinner with me.'

Olivia shook her head. 'I'm sorry, I can't. I was out last night and I'm out again tomorrow. I need an evening at home.' To make the refusal more gracious, she added, 'May I offer you a cup of coffee?'

'Thank you.' He shrugged off his coat, looking round for somewhere to put it in the small lobby.

'In here.' She opened a cupboard with a hanging rail. 'What were you doing in the corridors of power?'

'I was with a delegation of owners of large listed houses, trying yet again to prevail on government officials to make our repairs tax deductible. As it isn't a vote-grabbing issue, we're unlikely ever to succeed. How was your day?'

'More amusing than yours. I had lunch with the leader of a pop group, who looks maniacal on stage but is unexpectedly civilised in private. He's bought himself a very nice Regency house and wants me to redesign the interior.'

As she led the way into her living-room, Ludovic glanced round and said drily, 'One would never guess this room had just been redecorated.'

Olivia had temporarily forgotten her pretext for not inviting him up the previous week. With as much aplomb as she could muster, she said, 'A successful décor should never look new. . .even if it's only a room-set at an exhibition. Do sit down. I won't be a minute.'

Before going to her tiny kitchen, she switched off the lamp illuminating her drawing-table and turned the drawing face-down. She did not want him to see it until it was finished.

When she returned with the coffee-tray, Ludovic was scanning the titles of her books. 'I hear you've bought some of Hattie Frost's pictures,' he said. 'And you wrote a very nice thank-you note to Annette. She was delighted with the labels you sent her.'

'I had them in my present drawer and they seemed an appropriate token of my appreciation. Hattie told me Mrs Trent did a lot of preserving and bottling.'

'It's one of her hobbies. What do you do for relaxation, Olivia?'

'Trawl antiques shops. . .browse in museums. Most of my pastimes have a link with my work. What do you do?'

'I like rock-climbing, and I've a boat berthed on the south coast. In summer, I sometimes take a day or weekend to go sailing. I'm trying to work out a system that will keep the college running smoothly when I'm absent for longer periods. The fact that we're open all year round is a complication.'

Olivia poured out the coffee. 'When the system is in place, where will you go and for how long?'

'To some of the islands in the sun where we sailed when I was a boy. I'd like to be able to take off for a month or six weeks.'

'Won't the places be changed. . .no longer the way you remember them?'

'Some of them, yes. But the world still has a lot of unspoilt corners off-limits to package tourists.' He put up a hand. 'Before you jump in and tell me that tourists have as much right to see the world as I have, I don't dispute it. I just don't want to be surrounded by them when I'm getting away from it all.'

'I don't either,' she admitted. 'Tell me about some places that you wouldn't expect to have been spoilt.'

Unlike Mark, who seized any opportunity to hold forth at interminable length on subjects dear to his heart, Ludovic talked with enthusiasm, but not for long.

'Have you already eaten?' he asked suddenly.

'No, I'll have a sandwich later.'

'I don't want to dine on my own. If you're not in the mood to come out, why not let me make an omelette for both of us while you finish what you're doing?'

Disconcerted, she said, 'I think you'd have a problem finding your way round my kitchen.'

'Try me.' There was a challenge in the way he was looking at her.

She suspected that what he was expecting was for her to allow him to stay, but with her preparing the supper rather than having to tell him where everything was kept and finding, at the end of his culinary efforts, that her kitchen was a shambles.

'All right,' she agreed. 'But on two conditions.'

'Name them.'

'That you do it without disturbing me, and you clean up the mess.'

'When men make remarks like that, they're accused of being sexist. There won't be any mess,' he said confidently, getting up to take off the jacket of his city suit—not the same one he had worn last time.

She watched him unlink his shirt-cuffs and fold them back to mid-way up his sinewy forearms. What a fool she had been to agree to this. Now her quiet evening was in ruins. She would never be able to recover her concentration with him rooting about in the kitchen cupboards and drawers.

And what did he have in mind when supper was over?

For the next forty-five minutes Olivia sat at her drawing-table, trying to continue the work he had interrupted but with more than half her mind on what was going on behind the closed door of the kitchen. It would have taken her about ten minutes to make an omelette. Even allowing for the fact that he had to locate everything, from the eggs to the pepper grinder, it seemed to be taking him an inordinately long time.

She was on the point of going to investigate when Ludovic opened the kitchen door and announced, 'Dinner is about to be served, madam. On a tray, on your lap.'

She was in her favourite armchair, expecting to have to be polite about something resembling a wash-leather, when he brought her a tray on which a triangular slice of hot Spanish omelette was garnished with fried button mushrooms and accompanied by green salad, hot rusks and a glass of rosé.

'I assumed you were giving me carte blanche to use whatever I could find,' he said, returning with his own tray.

Olivia unfolded the white paper napkin he had put on the side-plate. 'Who would have thought a New Man lurked inside that very macho exterior?'

Ludovic looked amused. 'A lot of sailing men are New Men. If they don't learn certain skills, life can be pretty uncomfortable. When your sex are banging on about what a rotten lot men are, they should remember a lot of our behaviour was instilled when we were children. Women have the power to change men, not as their partners—by then it's too late—but as their mothers.'

'Mmm. . .this is a great omelette,' said Olivia, after tasting a forkful. 'I see now why you seemed to be taking a long time. You had to boil the potatoes and fry some onion.'

'I can only cook four or five things, this being one of them. That's a very neat kitchen in there. The layout is logical and a hygiene inspector couldn't fault you for cleanliness.'

'I can only take credit for the design. I have a weekly cleaner who does the housework.'

'Did she come today?'

'She'll be here tomorrow.'

'Then you have to be naturally tidy. The whole place looks immaculate,' he said, glancing round the room.

'Isn't order a part of comfort? I couldn't relax in a mess.'

'I see you also have *Visions of Paradise*,' he said, referring back to his survey of her books. 'Does that mean you're a frustrated gardener?'

'Not really. Ideally, I'd like a penthouse with a small roof-garden, but I don't know if I have green fingers or not. *Visions of Paradise* was a present from a satisfied customer who is a passionate gardener. To me, it's a beautifully illustrated coffee-table book I enjoy browsing through from time to time.'

While they ate, they talked about other books he had noticed on her shelves. It was a safe subject and one she enjoyed discussing, putting to the back of her mind the possibility that he might be deliberately building a feeling of harmony before making a determined pass at her.

CHAPTER SEVEN

BUT if that was his plan, it surprised Olivia that, on the 'liquor is quicker' principle, Ludovic didn't replenish her wine-glass when, some time after he finished his, she drained the last of her rosé.

Instead, he said, 'You go back to work while I carry out the second condition.'

This time he left the kitchen door open, and she could hear the water running and the sound of things being replaced where they belonged. In all the time she had known Mark, he had never so much as heated a take-out pizza. He was the perfect example of the son of an indulgent mother. Olivia had always known that, if she'd had flu or broken a leg, Mark's reaction would be to send flowers and make sympathetic noises on the telephone, not to come round and cosset her in the way Ludovic appeared to be capable of doing.

At this moment, after eating his supper and having an enjoyable chat, she could have liked him very much—if his entry into her life had been last week, not nine years ago. There was no way around that stumbling block.

Presently the aroma of coffee drifted through and she guessed he was using the percolator she kept for dinner parties. When he returned, he said, 'Can't I persuade you to take a weekend off and come down to Ramillies tomorrow night? You know what they say about all work and no play.'

'My work is a lot more enjoyable than most

people's,' she said, returning to the sitting area, but this time choosing a chair rather than one end of the sofa. 'It's nice of you to suggest it, but I can't get away this weekend. On Saturday I'm going to the wedding of the daughter of a tycoon. When she was coming up to sixteen, and away at school, he had me re-do her bedroom as a surprise for her birthday. He's a very indulgent father and the wedding is sure to be spectacular. But she's only nineteen. I'm afraid it may be the first step in her father's footsteps. He's just had his third divorce.'

'Have you met the bridegroom?'

Olivia shook her head. 'I hope he's in love with her, not with Daddy's millions.'

As if he were the host, and she the guest, Ludovic placed a cup of coffee and the cream jug on the small table next to her chair. Looking down at her, he said, 'Let's hope Daddy doesn't see you as the fourth Mrs Tycoon and decide that his daughter's wedding is the appropriate moment to sweep you off your feet.'

Olivia laughed. 'If you'd seen photographs of the previous Mrs Tycoons, you'd know that I don't qualify in any particular. Even if I did, I shouldn't be tempted. He's fifty, about five feet five, and his waist measurement must be nearly the same as his age. And even if he weren't egg-shaped, his track record isn't encouraging.'

Ludovic returned to the sofa. He was still in his shirt-sleeves and the light from the lamp behind his left shoulder emphasised the long, lean lines of his tall, virile body, which didn't need to be backed by material possessions to make it desirable to women. Long before he inherited Ramillies, he would have been drawing women's eyes to those broad, muscular shoulders and long, rangy legs.

From the safe distance of her chair, she could feel his magnetism working on her, filling her mind with thoughts of what it would be like to be curled on the sofa close to that powerful frame which, in the literal sense, could easily sweep her off her feet. And perhaps in the other sense as well, if she didn't watch out. He had an unnerving way of taking control of situations.

He did it now when he said, 'Shall we watch the news? And then I'll be on my way.'

'Yes. . .if you like.' She got up to switch on the television and pick up the remote control, relieved that he obviously wasn't intending to stay late, even hoping to stay all night.

Then she realised she wouldn't be able to see the screen from where she had been sitting. She would have to move to the sofa, where she usually sat to watch TV. Was that why he had suggested it? As an easy way to place her in a position where he could make a smoother pass?

The night's main news was political, with shots of a vociferous row in the House of Commons followed by interviews with selected MPs, one of them Mark. Watching him made her wonder how she could ever have thought their futures lay together.

But when Ludovic said, 'I can't stand this posturing idiot,' she found herself answering defensively.

'He's considered very bright. . .a possible future Prime Minister.'

'God help Britain if he ever makes it.'

While Mark held forth on the screen, Ludovic linked his fingers behind his head and watched him through narrowed eyes, the curl at the corner of his mouth an indication of his response to what the MP was saying.

His air of being totally at home in her flat, and totally contemptuous of someone for whom she would always have some kindly feelings, put Olivia's back up.

She said brusquely, 'He's doing more for his country than you are.'

'That's debatable. He's a power-hunter. . .as they all are. I dislike politicians of every persuasion.' He lifted an eyebrow. 'You're not a signed-up supporter of any of the parties, are you?'

She shook her head. 'But I've met this MP, and he does have some good ideas and worthwhile intentions.'

'They all have some good ideas, but they waste too much of their energy—and bore the pants off the voters—sniping at each other,' said Ludovic. 'Where did you meet him?' he asked, as Mark's face was replaced by that of another young politico.

'At a party. . . It was several years ago. He wasn't as well known then. He——'

She broke off as, suddenly, Ludovic moved from the other end of the sofa to its centre, picking up the zapper as he did so and pressing the button which made the screen go blank.

The next moment she was in his arms and he was stroking her hair away from her face and saying quietly, 'There are better things to do than listen to all that hot air. This week has seemed like a month to me. Has it to you?'

Then, without waiting for her answer, he began to kiss her; not with the unequivocal message of his previous kisses in the library, when she had felt his desire like the heat of a furnace, but with a tenderness which threw her into confusion.

She hadn't been kissed like this since her first embraces with Tom, long ago in Bali. Soft, loving kisses on her eyelids, while his fingertips traced exploratory paths from her temples to the base of her throat.

It was his gentleness which threw her, undermining her resistance and stirring an answering tenderness. Against her intentions, she found her free arm creeping up to circle his shoulders, delighting in their solid strength.

It wasn't until his lips found their way to her mouth that alarm bells began to ring in the back of her mind, becoming louder and more urgent as his hold on her tightened and the kiss became more demanding.

But it was when she felt him touching her breast, a caress that even with a layer of lambswool and a bra between his hand and her flesh sent a shiver of pleasure through her, that she knew she must stop this. . .*now*!

Once she had made that clear, he didn't try to restrain her. It would have been easy for him to keep her in his arms, but he didn't. He let her go. And Olivia made sure she didn't weaken by jumping to her feet and grabbing the coffee-tray.

Holding it in front of her, she said unsteadily, 'I really don't think it's a good idea for us to do that sort of thing if we're going to be involved professionally.'

'I don't see why not. . .if neither of us has any conflicting relationships. I'm free. Aren't you?'

'Yes, but that isn't the issue. You're a prospective client. Business and pleasure don't mix.'

Ludovic was on his feet now. He gave her a long, searching look.

'In general, maybe not. But none of my other

business relationships is with a woman like you. . .to whom I'm strongly attracted. You may not want to admit it, but you feel the same. So why do we have to pretend there isn't a mutual attraction?'

Because you're the last man in the world I want to feel that way about.

But if she said that, he would demand to know why, and the explanation would really put the kibosh on their professional connection.

Searching for a get-out that he would find acceptable, she said, 'I was attracted to Kevin Costner when I saw him in *Dances with Wolves*. It doesn't mean we would have anything in common if we met. Attractions are notoriously insubstantial and ephemeral. You and I hardly know each other.'

'To me it feels as if we've known each other a long time.'

'You may feel that way. . . I don't,' she said firmly. 'I need to know someone a much longer time before. . .before. . .' Why did he make her flounder for words like a schoolgirl?

'Before you'll let them make love to you?' he suggested.

'Yes.' Finding it hard to meet the amused blue eyes, she turned and carried the tray into the kitchen.

He followed her, standing in the doorway while she washed out the cups. 'I'm reading your lips, Olivia, but the words they're saying don't tally with the way they felt against mine a few minutes ago. Nor do I believe you're a woman who never plays hunches. . . never acts on impulse. Tonight is the second time you've been soft and warm in my arms. Why not trust your instincts? Let the woman overrule the businesswoman?'

'They're not in conflict,' she said coolly. 'I prefer being in charge of my life. . .not being ruled by facile emotions.'

As she reached for the teatowel he moved closer, taking her by the shoulders and turning her to face him.

'Women as lovely as you don't usually keep their feelings on ice. I think somebody has to have hurt you, but that isn't my intention. Why not tell me what happened?'

'Nothing happened. I'm just out of step with people who jump into bed at the first buzz of attraction. I need to know and trust someone before I get to that stage, and you and I are virtually strangers. Actually, you're the one who's out of step, Ludovic. Most intelligent women feel the way I do.'

'I won't argue with that, but you're backing off prematurely. I haven't tried to rush you into bed,' he said drily.

'That seemed to be where we were heading if I hadn't backed off. As long as I'm visiting Ramillies on a professional basis, I'd rather we kept things friendly. . .without complications.'

There was a short and, for Olivia, tense pause, before he said, 'All right. If that's the way you want it. But I still think I'm right about the reason for your keeping your feelings battened down to this extent. Hopefully there'll be a point when you trust me enough to tell me about it. Meanwhile. . .'

With a shrug, he returned to the sitting-room.

Olivia had already dried her wet hands on the towel. Leaving the cups until later, she went to the cupboard in the lobby to get out his raincoat.

'Thank you for my supper,' she said politely, holding it for him to put on.

'Thank you for the freedom of your kitchen,' he replied, with an ironic bow. 'I'll look forward to the night when you trust me enough to admit me to your bedroom, Olivia. Meanwhile, we'll play it your way. But a goodnight kiss is allowable in the most strait-laced circles.'

He took her face between his hands and bent to kiss her mouth.

With their lips an inch apart, he said, in a mocking murmur, 'You belong in my arms, and you know it. This is only a postponement. I won't say "sleep well", because I know you won't. Nor shall I. But your frustration will be of your own making.'

The slow kiss he pressed on her lips made sure that after he had gone, as she leaned against her front door, every fibre of her body was clamouring for her to rush out and call him back.

'They're the best you've ever done,' said Grace, the first person to see the Ramillies visualisations. 'But you look done in,' she added.

'Burning the midnight oil doesn't suit me,' said Olivia, shrugging. 'But I wanted to get these finished. I'd like to have the Ramillies contract safely in the bag.'

That hadn't been the only reason why, for two nights running, she had worked until four and five in the morning on the storyboards Grace was admiring. She wouldn't have slept if she had gone to bed.

With that last profoundly sensual kiss, Ludovic had reached into the depths of her being and ignited a fire which, even now, when she was almost exhausted, was still smouldering.

'Have these colour-copied and packaged and tell Freddy we have an urgent job for him, will you?' she said to her PA.

Freddy was an independent motorcycle courier they often used to run urgent errands around London.

That afternoon, crossing Hyde Park in a taxi after a buffet lunch presentation by the German manufacturers of luxury kitchen units, Olivia asked the driver to drop her on the bridge across the Serpentine. It was a lovely afternoon and she felt the need for some fresh air—or what passed for it here in the heart of London—and brisk exercise.

Following the path round the lake, looking at the daffodils under the trees, she couldn't help thinking of the park and the woods at Ramillies, where every year the drifts of spring flowers multiplied.

By now the results of her midnight-oil sessions should be on their way to their destination. She knew they deserved Grace's accolade. They *were* the best things she had done. Her intimate knowledge of the house and her special feeling for it had inspired her. She was certain Ludovic would be impressed.

Ludovic. The thought of him was a torment she didn't know how to deal with. What did he want from her? A brief affair? A longer but equally impermanent relationship, like his liaisons with the college art teacher and the horsewoman? Or could it be that he too was at an age when a serious commitment offered more satisfaction, but so far he had failed to find the right person to commit to?

All she knew was that, since the other night, she couldn't stop thinking about him, wondering how it would have been if, instead of losing her nerve when their embrace on the sofa had threatened to become too passionate, she had let things take their course.

One thing was certain. If Ludovic's prowess as a lover could be judged by the effect of his kisses, she would not have lain awake afterwards, restless and unfulfilled, as she had many times with Mark.

With Tom it had all been different. They had both been so young, so new to love, that everything had been wonderful. They had lain in each other's arms in a palm-thatched hut close to a Balinese beach and it had been heaven just to hold him and feel his heart thudding against hers. She hadn't asked for anything more.

With Mark she had had different expectations, and that was what they had remained. Unfulfilled hopes. Unexpressed longings. He had taken it for granted that he was marvellous in bed and she had never disillusioned him. Not that he would have believed her. He was not a man who suffered from much uncertainty about his capabilities in any sphere. In that respect, he and Ludovic had a good deal in common.

And, if she were fool enough to get involved with Ludovic in the way he wanted, she might find that after a while, like Mark, he would drop her.

She was in bed, half-asleep with a book in her hands, when he rang up to say, 'They're brilliant, Olivia. All I expected and more. There's no need to discuss them. They're perfect. Go ahead with the estimates, will you?'

He was not on the line for long. After singling out three or four aspects of her proposals for more detailed praise, he said goodnight and rang off.

Olivia replaced the book on the stack on her bedside table and lay down, leaving the light on so that she could see her most treasured possession, the personal bequests left to her by Ludovic's great-uncle.

The one she loved best was the Regency *bonheur-du-jour*, bought for a Webb wife or daughter to use for writing letters to her sons or brothers, several of whom, when the desk had been new, had been fighting Napoleon in Spain and France. Olivia valued it all the more because it had been her reward for not smoking or drinking, and it symbolised Rathbone's confidence that if she set out to do something—or, as in this case, not to do something—she had the determination to follow through, no matter how difficult it might be to resist the temptation to go with the crowd.

On the wall above the desk hung a needlework picture from the same period, a map of the counties of England outlined in once-bright sewing silks now faded to softer tones by the light of nearly two centuries.

His third bequest was the box on her dressing-table. With it, in a secret drawer but itemised in Rathbone's will, had been the jewellery he had left her, including the cameo ring she had taken off to go to Ramillies.

It was on her night-table now, removed before she'd had her bath. For the first time it struck her that she must have been wearing it the other night when Ludovic had called at the flat unexpectedly. Could he have noticed it without recognising the crest? Or, having passed first base in the library at Ramillies, had he been too intent on reaching home plate and scoring to be aware of such details?

It was the bursar at the college, Geoffrey Brewster, with whom Olivia had most to do during the next stage. Faxes flew back and forth between his office and hers and they had several lengthy telephone discussions. He was a pleasant man to deal with.

When all the financial aspects had been agreed, Ludovic rang her up. She didn't know whether he had been away or had been deliberately avoiding further personal contact.

After some polite preliminaries, he said, 'I thought we might celebrate the signing of the contract with a dinner *à quatre* at the Nabob with Geoffrey and Annette.'

Normally Olivia would have delegated a great deal of the work to her staff and would have suggested including at least two of them in any celebration. But this time she had dealt with almost everything herself, as she had had to in the early days.

After they had fixed a mutually convenient date, Ludovic concluded the conversation with a briskness she found oddly deflating. Maybe someone more alluring than herself had crossed his path, or perhaps there was truth in the rumours about his relationship with Annette and he was beginning to feel he could do a lot worse than marry her.

A few days later Olivia had a call from Bonnie Westmacott who, with Tyler, was coming to Europe for the wedding of Tyler's favourite cousin to an Italian. The ceremony would be in Rome, but they had arranged to spend a night in London en route.

To Olivia's dismay, it was the same night she had already marked in her diary 'Nabob—7.00 for 7.30'. There being no way Bonnie could alter her arrangements, Olivia said she would be delighted to see them. Changing the date of the Nabob dinner shouldn't be a problem.

But it turned out that it was. Ludovic had several evening engagements that week and was going to be away the following week.

'Rather than putting off our foursome, at considerable inconvenience to everyone—Annette has a hair appointment at some fashionable place in Sloane Street—why not bring your American friends to the Nabob?' he suggested. 'I'm sure they'll enjoy it.'

'I'm sure they would, but I couldn't impose them on you.'

'Nonsense,' he said briskly. 'I'm sure any friends of yours will be interesting people. That's settled, then. Until the seventeenth. . . Goodbye, Olivia.'

Olivia did not go to the airport to meet the Westmacotts. She had an important meeting that morning, and anyway their Concorde flight across the Atlantic would be met by a limousine organised by Tyler's secretary, who masterminded all their travels.

Now in his late forties, Tyler was a senior partner in one of America's most prestigious law firms and he and his family enjoyed a life of considerable luxury but were still the same loving partners and parents they had been when Olivia first knew them.

She had sent a long fax to Bonnie via Tyler's office, explaining the situation and stressing that their host at the Nabob dinner party knew nothing of her previous connection with Ramillies and that, at this stage, she preferred to keep it under wraps.

She knew Tyler might not like being party to any kind of devious behaviour but that Bonnie would convince him there must be some good reason for asking them not to reveal the circumstances which had linked their lives with Olivia's.

Although she had written to Bonnie regularly since her year with them, Olivia had glossed over the events following what should have been her home-coming. At that time Bonnie had been in low spirits herself, following a miscarriage, and Olivia hadn't wanted to burden her with any of the unhappiness of her return to England. Nor had she ever said much about it when they had met in New York or when Bonnie had come to London.

The Westmacotts always stayed at the Savoy, where Tyler's parents had honeymooned during World War II and his elder sister had been conceived.

Olivia arrived at the hotel at six o'clock, and it was a measure of their standing with the hotel's management that she was conducted to their suite on the river side of the building by a dapper assistant manager.

Bonnie was looking beautiful in an apricot silk suit which set off her rich chestnut hair and tawny eyes and Tyler, although prematurely grey, was still in great shape for a man with his fiftieth birthday on the horizon.

They greeted Olivia with their usual heart-warming affection and she was eager to hear the latest news of the children, who were now around the age she had been when she first went to America.

But, after the family news up-date, it didn't surprise her when Tyler said, 'Olly, this business of pretending we've never heard of Ramillies could be a little tricky. Don't you think you should have come clean with Mr Webb? Doesn't this. . .this masquerade bother you?'

'It isn't much of a masquerade, Tyler, and I will come clean with him as soon as I can. But the row we had nine years ago, when he knew me as Olly Jones, has no bearing on the present situation. This contract is very important to me. Two of my clients were involved in the Lloyds disaster. They're going to be in debt for the rest of their lives. There's no way they can ever pay what they owe me. I had to write off a huge amount of money and it really set the business back. The Ramillies contract is a godsend and it's only the beginning. Ludovic's planned renovations will take years to complete.'

'Don't worry, Olly,' said Bonnie. 'We won't give the game away. . .and we'll make sure we call you Olivia,' she added. 'I'm not surprised Mr Webb has no idea who you are. You changed out of all recognition while you were living with us, but you've changed a lot more from the way you were in those photographs you and Kate sent back from your trip. I hunted them out the other day and brought a few with me. They're in my purse.'

She opened her elegant evening bag and produced the prints.

Tyler looked over Olivia's shoulder as she studied the shots of herself and her travelling companion with their arms round each other's shoulders as they beamed at whoever they had asked to photograph them. She had duplicates stored somewhere, but it was a long time since she had looked at these reminders of how she had been the first time Ludovic met her.

'You still had a lot of growing up to do when those were taken,' Tyler said. 'You were a couple of cute kids, but nobody would have guessed you were two top career women in the making.'

'Kate doesn't dress the way you do,' said Bonnie, with an appreciative gesture at Olivia's chic black dress and dramatic gold jewellery. 'But her life as a TV news reporter doesn't call for glamour. As you don't have satellite TV, I taped some of her recent reports for you.'

It was typical of her thoughtfulness. Bonnie was one of those rare beings who was always thinking of ways to please her family, friends and even casual acquaintances. It was she who had introduced Olivia to the idea of keeping a drawer stocked with presents, such as the labels she had given to Annette.

That Annette's afternoon in the hands of a London hairstylist had improved her slightly frumpy image was the first thing Olivia registered when the six of them met at the Nabob Club.

Annette also appeared to have lost a few pounds in weight and was wearing a printed silk shirt with a hip-diminishing black skirt. She looked several years younger and there was a glow in her eyes which had not been there the last time Olivia had seen her.

After the introductions, and while they were having drinks, Ludovic talked to Bonnie, Tyler made himself agreeable to Annette and Olivia forced herself to concentrate on Geoffrey Brewster and not allow her eyes to stray in the direction of their host.

Shaking hands with him had sent a tingle up her arm. For a moment she had thought he was going to lean forward and give her a social kiss on the cheek. But he hadn't, and she had a sinking feeling that she might never feel his lips again. Though that should be a relief, not a disappointment.

'I'm impressed by your grasp of the financial side of things, Miss Hartley,' said the bursar. 'In my experience, creative people are not usually very good at reading balance sheets. But clearly they hold no mysteries for you.'

'When I was starting up, I took evening classes in book-keeping and business management,' she explained. 'I also have a very good accountant. Perhaps you're also a member of the Institute?'

He nodded. 'I had to train for a new career after I lost the lower part of my left arm while I was in the Army.'

For the first time Olivia noticed that the hand projecting from his left sleeve was enclosed in a tight leather glove. She found Geoffrey a pleasant companion, but couldn't help feeling on edge in case either of the Westmacotts inadvertently let slip a reference to her as 'Olly'. She still wasn't sure if Ludovic had noticed the cameo and that was the reason for the change in his manner.

They had dinner at a round table in a small private room. With Geoffrey and Tyler on either side of her, and Bonnie and Annette flanking Ludovic, Olivia found herself seated directly opposite him.

The champagne they had drunk on arrival was followed by more champagne with the meal, which began with oyster *beignets*, the golden-brown batter light and crunchy in contrast to the creamy smoothness of the tartare sauce.

Conversation was general, with everyone contributing their experiences of Italy where the Westmacotts would be tomorrow. Annette and her husband had rented a villa there. Ludovic had sailed the west coast. Before she was married, Bonnie had spent six months there, studying the history of art.

When it was Olivia's turn to describe a hilarious incident during the doing up of a holiday house in Tuscany, she was aware, as she talked, of Ludovic's eyes on her.

While they were eating Irish sea-caged salmon cooked with ginger and rhubarb, she noticed that, probably mindful of the drive back to Ramillies, he was drinking sparingly. Annette was drinking too fast. It was making her giggly. She was going to wake up with a headache tomorrow, thought Olivia.

It annoyed her to think of Ludovic dropping Geoffrey at his house in the village and then taking Annette home and spending the night there. She didn't want to imagine him removing that silk blouse and the underpinnings beneath it and disarranging the expensive London coiffure. Suddenly she realised that her feelings were remarkably similar to the symptoms of jealousy, an emotion she had always despised. But jealousy sprang from love, and she didn't love Ludovic. She was attracted to him, yes. But love was something else: a complex combination of friendship, trust and respect. She did respect his achievement at Ramillies, but she didn't trust him, and there could never be friendship between them.

CHAPTER EIGHT

AFTER the arrival of the pudding, a spectacular pyramid of profiteroles veiled with caramelised sugar and served with butterscotch sauce, and when everyone's glass had been replenished, Ludovic said, 'It's time we drank to the reason for this occasion. I'm delighted that Tyler and Bonnie have been able to share it with us and we wish them a very happy time in Italy. Tonight, as you know, we're celebrating another significant stage in the renaissance of Ramillies, long the private house of a privileged family and now a place where each year hundreds of people enrich their lives with new skills and enjoy the beauty of the house and garden.'

Until he paused, he had been using the experienced speaker's technique of moving his gaze from listener to listener. Now, for the first time, he looked at Olivia.

'The glories of the interiors at Ramillies are about to be greatly enhanced by the skills of a designer who, after only one brief visit, has demonstrated an intuitive grasp of what's needed. The difficulty of renovating an old house was exemplified by the furore over the renovations at Althorp, Earl Spencer's historic house, a few years ago. I'm confident that when Olivia's designs are seen by the experts in such matters, there won't be any disagreement. Everyone will be as impressed as I am. Let's drink to a long and fruitful liaison between Olivia Hartley Designs and Ramillies College.'

After the first few moments, Olivia had looked at her lap. But she raised her eyes when he came to the formal toast and found him still looking at her with an enigmatic expression she could not interpret.

'Aren't you going to reply, Olivia?' Tyler asked, after everyone had raised their glasses—Annette with a murmured 'Whoops!' as the flourish of her gesture slopped some champagne over the rim of her glass.

'My skills don't include our host's mastery of the art of combining grace with brevity. Thank you for your kind words, Ludovic,' she said, raising her glass to him before taking another small sip.

With the coffee came liqueurs and exquisite fruit-flavoured fondants which lived up to their name by melting on the tongue. The one Olivia chose had the deliciously fugitive taste of a juicy midsummer raspberry.

Although the conversation showed no sign of abating, it was not quite eleven when Ludovic diplomatically but effectively brought the evening to a close.

The women had left their wraps in the cloakroom on the ground floor and it occurred to Olivia that, although Annette didn't look unsteady on her feet, it might be a good idea for someone to take her arm if they went down the beautiful circular staircase they had walked up earlier.

Perhaps Ludovic had had the same thought. He said, 'We'll go down in the lift.'

But when the lift doors opened, and Bonnie and Annette stepped in, he stopped Olivia from following them with a light touch on her arm. 'I want a quick word with Olivia,' he said to the two other men. 'The lift only holds four. She and I will follow you down in a moment.'

'Why don't we walk down?' she suggested, as the others disappeared from view.

'As you wish.' As they moved towards the staircase, which swept upwards in two further coils lit by day with a glass dome and tonight by graceful gilt and crystal sconces, he said, 'You were rather quiet this evening. Is anything wrong?'

'On the contrary. . . I was enjoying myself. But perhaps not contributing as much as a good guest should.'

He took her by the elbow and halted her. 'Even if you didn't open your mouth, you'd contribute a great deal of visual pleasure. If that's an example of the famous "little black dress", it's a knock-out.' His glance took in the neckline, designed to give a discreet glimpse of the hollow between her breasts.

'Thank you. . .and thank you for a marvellous evening. The food was delicious and I wish I had a tape of your speech to keep among my mementoes.'

'I like your friends very much. Would they like to come to stay at Ramillies for a night or two on their way back from Italy, do you think?'

Olivia knew they would both be delighted, but she said, 'I think they have various commitments which would make that impossible this time. Perhaps the next time they're——'

Her answer ended with a sharp intake of breath as she realised she was about to be kissed.

For some seconds the world blanked out and, instinctively closing her eyes, she was conscious of nothing but the warm, compelling mouth on hers.

Then up the wide stairwell came the voices of the others as they emerged from the lift on the ground floor. She opened her eyes and drew back.

'That wasn't fair.'

He lifted an eyebrow. 'Fair? What do you mean?'

She knew what she meant but was unable to explain. It didn't make for lucid explanations, being kissed by Ludovic.

Fortunately they were on the side of the staircase nearer to the wall than the graceful wrought-iron balustrade, where the treads were at their widest. She thought it unlikely the kiss had been seen from below.

With him still holding her arm, they continued down. 'Why wasn't it fair?' he persisted.

'Because I'm your guest. . .and I've already told you I don't want to complicate things.'

'It might simplify them.'

'I don't understand you.'

'Nor I you, Olivia,' he said drily. 'As I've already told you, your body language doesn't match what you say.'

He took his hand from her arm to place it against her back, just above the waist. Then it slid slightly lower, his fingers moving caressingly, making her insides clench.

She felt an impulse to swing round and bring her palm into stinging contact with his face. But it was a reaction which both the old men who had raised her would have regarded with horror. Not all, but a lot of their manners and mores still governed her behaviour. More to the point, it would have been hypocritical. You couldn't slap a man's face for doing something which made you burn with desire for him to do more.

Tyler and Geoffrey were alone when they joined them, the women having gone to retrieve their wraps from the cloakroom. When she joined them there,

Olivia was surprised to find Bonnie and Annette discussing hormone replacement therapy.

Then some other women came in and Annette disappeared into one of the cubicles.

Under cover of the others' voices, Bonnie murmured, 'She had a hot flush in the elevator. I noticed, but the men didn't. She's going through the menopause and getting no help at all from her physician.'

Remembering how, years ago, Bonnie had sorted out her problems for her, Olivia couldn't help wishing the two older women had had more time to chat. Everyone confided in Bonnie. She would soon have found out whether Ludovic was leading Annette up the garden path. Not because she would probe, but because there was something about her that invited such confidences.

When Ludovic said goodbye to Bonnie, he kissed her hand. He did not repeat the salute with Olivia. But as they shook hands he looked at her mouth, and she knew he was thinking about the kiss on the staircase. She felt he was bent on possessing her, and her reluctance to become involved with him was fuelling his determination.

The Westmacotts were not tired and wanted to see what changes Olivia had made to her apartment since their visit the year before.

'Why wasn't Mark included in tonight's party?' asked Bonnie, in the taxi.

'We've split up.'

'Whose idea was that? Yours?'

'No, his.'

'That *does* surprise me. I never thought you were in love with him, but he seemed serious about you.'

'He decided, very sensibly, that I wasn't cut out to

be a parliamentary wife. Which I'm not. I'm not sure I want to be anyone's wife.'

Bonnie reached out and took her hand in an affectionate clasp. 'Yes, you do. You just haven't met the right man yet. All women want to be loved and needed. I don't underestimate the satisfactions of a successful career, but you need to be a wife and mother as well, Olly. You have a lot of love to give.'

'What did you think of Ludovic?' Olivia asked Tyler, who was facing them from one of the jump-seats.

'He seemed a nice guy,' was his non-committal answer.

'*Very* attractive,' said his wife. 'Has he been married?'

'Not that I know of.'

'Annette's crazy about him, but I don't think she has a hope,' said Bonnie.

'According to local gossip, she may be his mistress.'

'If she is, that's all she'll ever be. He's not in love with her.'

'I'd agree with that,' said her husband.

'Why?' Olivia asked him.

Tyler smiled at her. 'I don't have this women's intuition that Bonnie has so much faith in, and I wouldn't claim to be as observant as you girls, who never miss a nuance, but I'm reasonably observant. While Annette was focused on him, Ludovic was focused on you, Olly.'

'Only because that was the point of the dinner.'

'I think not,' he said firmly. 'He has a personal interest in you. But unlike this sentimental soul——' he reached forward to lay an affectionate hand on his wife's knee '—I don't assume he must have marriage

in mind. I would think any man who has escaped the
net at his age has decided he doesn't need a wife.'

Ignoring his provocative reference to the net,
Bonnie said, 'With that beautiful house to hand on to
future generations, he needs a wife more than most.
For that reason alone, he wouldn't marry Annette.
She should have the sense to know that.'

'Perhaps she sees the role of a wife as something
more than a brood mare?' said Olivia. 'I'm sure you
wouldn't have married Tyler if you'd thought his
principal interest was begetting another generation of
the Westmacott dynasty.'

'No, but I knew he wanted children, and if I'd had
any doubts about my ability to have them, I would
have declared them,' Bonnie said seriously. 'Family
traditions. . .family values are very important. If
Ludovic *isn't* planning to marry and raise children,
he's avoiding the responsibilities of his position.
Noblesse oblige, and all that.'

'I shouldn't think he gives a damn about *noblesse
oblige*,' said Olivia. 'He strikes me as a dedicated
egoist.'

'If he were that, wouldn't he have sold the house?'
said Tyler. 'From everything you've told us, it was
very run-down when he took it over.'

'He almost did sell it. I expect the reason he didn't
was because he liked the VIP status ownership of
Ramillies conferred on him.'

'That's not the impression I received,' said Tyler.
'He was talking about it while we were waiting for
you. He's set up a trust to keep the place going
whether or not he has heirs. But from the way he
spoke it sounded as if, once he's seen this final phase

of renovations accomplished, he might not stay at Ramillies.'

'Where will he go?' asked Bonnie.

'He's a qualified yachtmaster. He may go back to sea. He's spent most of his life on a deck.'

'Hmm. . .that doesn't make him a good bet from a woman's point of view,' was her comment. 'Men with itchy feet or the sea in their veins should stay single. Their nomadic instincts conflict with our nesting instincts.'

The taxi drew up outside the entrance to the flats and Tyler sprang out and helped the two women alight before paying the fare. Although the Westmacotts stayed with Olivia till midnight, Ludovic wasn't mentioned again.

The following day was a busy one for Olivia. She had a sandwich lunch at her desk and in the evening went to a meeting of a career women's network. Afterwards, she and two other members had a pasta supper at a trattoria in Soho, a locale close to London's theatreland, where the sleazy side of the city's night-life went on alongside inexpensive family-run foreign restaurants, avant-garde art galleries and shops full of tourist tat.

It wasn't until she got home and ran herself a bath, tossing some soluble capsules of her favourite extravagantly expensive French bath-oil into the stream from the hot tap, that she had time to examine the thought which, all day, had twinged like the mental equivalent of a tiny but painful splinter in one of her fingers. The thought of Ludovic leaving Ramillies and disappearing into the limitless vastness of the world's oceans.

As she lay in the warm scented water, looking at the

fragment of antique toile de Jouy she had had framed
to hang on the wall above the taps, she was forced to
recognise that there could be only one reason why the
possibility of Ludovic returning to his former life
should revive the pain she had felt on returning from
Guatemala to find her world turned upside-down.

Somehow, against her will, she had fallen in love
with him. Which made the thought of his leaving
Ramillies unbearable.

The next day Hattie Frost rang up to invite her to
come to a party at the Old Barn Gallery the following
Saturday, staying overnight in their guest-room.

Taking Hattie's paintings back to the gallery to be
framed for the restaurant she was decorating was one
of the things on Olivia's current 'To Do' list. Having a
legitimate reason for going there made it easier to
succumb to the temptation to accept the invitation,
although common sense told her it was a mistake to go
anywhere where she stood a good chance of meeting
Ludovic socially.

She would have to encounter him professionally.
That was unavoidable. But she wouldn't have to stay
at Ramillies again. It was near enough to London for
her supervisory visits to be day-trips.

Having accepted the invitation, as the week pro-
gressed she found herself giving a good deal of thought
to what to wear. . .in case Ludovic should be at the
party. The illogicality of wanting to look her best for a
man she should be trying not to think about made her
angry with herself.

She remembered how, the day he came to her office,
she had told him she wanted everything life had to
offer a woman. At the time, it had been a corrective

to her previous statement that her work was her life. But now she knew it was true; she wanted more than her career. She wanted a satisfying private life which, at the moment, hers wasn't. Nor had it been right with Mark. Without love it could never be right. But why, dammit, had she had to go and fall in love with Ludovic Webb? Not only had he done the unforgivable but, from what he had told Tyler, it sounded as if he didn't mean to stay in England for much longer.

Driving down to the Old Barn, she thought, Maybe I should give him what he wants and get him out of my system.

But she knew she couldn't do that. She had loved Tom. She had liked and admired Mark. At the beginning he hadn't seemed as pompous and self-satisfied as he had turned out to be. It was too late in her life to start being a swinger. No-strings affairs weren't her style. She was ready for the big commitment.

She remembered what Ludovic had said about his parents. 'They had mated for life, as a few lucky people still do.'

He had also said that his mother had been exceptional and that girls like her, rare even then, were now extinct.

As she put the car into fifth gear and cruised at a steady sixty-five, Olivia found herself imagining what it would be like to sell up her business and start a new life as a sea-gypsy.

It might be fun for a few weeks, even a few months. But she knew that, for her, it wasn't a viable way of life. The cramped living quarters, the need to reduce one's possessions to a minimum, the physical discomforts and dangers which must be an integral part of any long ocean passage, were all anathema to her.

She could never adapt to that life. Not for anyone. It would be folly to attempt it. That was one of the many reasons why marriages fell apart. . .because people believed they could change their partners or themselves. She had seen it happen so often, with girlfriends and business contacts. They thought love would work wonders, but it didn't. If Ludovic's mother had really enjoyed her life at sea, she must have been a natural adventurer.

Olivia had enjoyed the adventures of the year before her return to Ramillies. But her personality hadn't been fully formed then. Now it was. She knew she needed to be loved as she was now. If and when she married, she would need to love her husband as *he* was. . .not as she might like him to be. Which made it even more foolish to find herself in love with Ludovic. Had he not behaved badly towards her grandfather, had he intended to spend his life at Ramillies and, most important of all, had he wanted to emulate his parents and mate for life, there might have been some future in loving him.

As things were, her only recourse was to tell herself this was merely an infatuation which, if she was sensible about it, would eventually wear off.

She was backing the car into a corner of the car park, to leave as much room as possible for the late arrivals, when Ben came out of the gallery.

Unexpectedly, he greeted her with a kiss on the cheek, which she thought was jumping the gun a bit. She preferred to shake hands until she knew people well and felt a good deal more warmly than she felt towards Ben. He was nice, but he wasn't a close friend.

'Hattie's very excited at having you to stay over-night,' he told her, lifting her case from the boot. 'Annette's been here most of the day, helping Hat with the catering. She says you haven't been to Ramillies since the weekend we met. I'd thought you'd be spending a lot of time there.'

'I made extensive notes, took lots of photographs and I have a good visual memory,' Olivia answered. 'When is your next framing course?'

'Not till August. I'd like to do six a year but Ludovic won't let me do more than three, even though my last one was full up. He's very dictatorial. Won't budge once he's made up his mind,' Ben said, with a grimace. 'As I expect you'll find out, he can be an obstinate cuss.'

'Is he coming tonight?'

'He said he might look in late, but I shouldn't be surprised if he doesn't. He's got some bigwigs staying, so probably won't deign to honour the likes of us with his presence.'

'You sound very anti, Ben. I thought you and Hattie liked Ludovic, and had a good relationship with him.'

'Hat's got a crush on him. So, I suspect, has Annette. He enjoys charming your sex. With mine, it's a different matter. . .unless they're VIPs. He doesn't waste charm on me. Whenever I've been to his office, it's been like a summons to see the headmaster.' He pushed open the door of the gallery for her. 'You may not have seen that aspect of him yet, and perhaps you won't. . .provided you keep on the right side of him.'

'What have you done to get on the wrong one?'

'Nothing that I know of. Anyway, let's forget Ludovic. Hopefully he'll be too busy with the visiting bigwigs to show up here tonight.'

Olivia knew she should try to share that hope. It would be much better for her peace of mind if Ludovic didn't put in an appearance.

By nine o'clock the party was under way. Hattie had a tray fixed to the arms of her chair so that she could wheel herself about, offering plates of delicious nibbles as a preliminary to supper due to be served at ten o'clock.

She was wearing a yellow T-shirt with a sparkly appliqué, designed by herself, on the front. She looked very pretty and animated.

'Have you heard from your American friends how their wedding in Italy went off?' Annette asked, when she and Olivia, who had both been taking round trays of *bouchées*, returned to the kitchen at the same time.

'Not yet. I expect Bonnie will write a long, detailed account of it as soon as she gets home.'

Annette, who was wearing the same blouse she had worn at the Nabob but appeared to have put back the pounds she had lost, helped herself to a miniature vol-au-vent.

'I had a dreadful headache the day after that dinner,' she confessed. 'I'm not used to champagne. It sent me to sleep on the way home. I shall stick to soft drinks tonight, as I'm driving myself. I hate driving at night. . .although not as much now that Ludovic has given me a mobile telephone. He says all women drivers should have them. He's very thoughtful in those ways.'

Ben came in with an empty bottle of wine in each

hand. 'You're not here to work, Olivia. You're supposed to be taking it easy.'

'I'm enjoying it,' she said, picking up the last tray of pastry boats filled with prawns in a spicy dressing. 'Helping to serve the snacks is a good way of getting to know people.'

As Annette returned to the gallery, he said, 'You look gorgeous in that outfit. Everyone's asking about you.'

'Thank you.'

After several changes of mind, Olivia had finally decided on a jump-suit made from a length of indigo and white batik-printed cotton from a firm whose imports she often used in decorating schemes. It was cool and casual, and wouldn't come to any harm when she helped with the clearing up afterwards. She had cinched her waist with a wide navy blue belt, tied a navy kerchief round her throat and added silver earrings and a jingle of silver bracelets to her left wrist.

'After supper we'll dance,' said Ben, gazing at her with a hungry expression she hoped didn't mean he was going to be a problem later.

'My dancing days are over. I never was much good at it. I prefer to watch,' she said firmly.

It was true. The kind of dancing that appealed to her was the white-tie-and-tails routines performed by Fred Astaire in fifty-year-old movies shown late at night on TV. Films like *The Barkleys of Broadway* could start her body moving to the ballroom and tap rhythms of long ago. She could identify with the girls in *A Chorus Line* and Liza Minelli in *Stepping Out*, but she didn't want to writhe and grind in the gallery with Ben.

If Ludovic came. . . If the music was slow and sweet. . .

She stamped on that thought, saying quickly, 'I must get back to my duties,' and hurrying back to the party.

At five minutes to ten she helped Annette to remove the long piece of French table-paper draped over the buffet.

Looking at the sumptuous spread, most of it from Annette's kitchen, she said, 'I don't know why you don't do this professionally. Your talents are wasted in the office at Ramillies. It wouldn't please Ludovic to hear me say so, but I'm sure you'd earn more cooking for parties, and your working hours would be more flexible.'

'You're right. . .it doesn't please Ludovic,' a voice said drily from the doorway, making Annette give a startled squeak and Olivia's heart do a flip.

As they turned, he gave a slight bow which included them both. 'Good evening. What are you doing, encouraging my staff to desert me, Olivia? Would you like it if I tried to lure your girl Grace away from you?'

His expression was inscrutable. She couldn't tell if he was teasing or serious.

'If working for you gave her more scope for her talents than she had with me, I hope I'd be pleased for her,' she said pleasantly. 'This——' with a gesture embracing the buffet '—is obviously Annette's *métier*.'

'I shoudn't dream of leaving my job at Ramillies,' Annette put in quickly. 'I love it there and I like to think that, although no one's indispensable, it might be difficult to find anyone *more* conscientious.'

Ludovic picked up his cue. 'Impossible. And, knowing you better than Olivia does, I doubt if you'd get as much pleasure out of catering professionally as you do out of helping friends with their parties. Running a business successfully calls for a certain ruthlessness, which I'm sure she has, when it's needed, but which isn't part of your temperament.'

Clearly Annette wasn't sure how to take this statement. Nor was Olivia. She said, 'I thought you weren't coming tonight. . .or only looking in later.'

'That was the plan. . .but I changed it.' He left it at that.

'Olivia, would you go and ask Ben to announce that supper is served?' said Annette.

'Of course.' She left them together, aware that it was as if all the lights in the building had been dimmed and were now switched to maximum power.

She had read about love making people feel more alive, and had herself experienced that sensation while she and Tom were both in the throes of first love. Against her will, she felt the same way tonight. On a stratospheric high. But she knew it was as illusory and dangerous as the highs induced by drugs. She had steered her life round *that* hazard. Was she going to let herself get hooked on an unsuitable man with almost equally disastrous effects?

Presently, sharing one of the gallery's cushioned benches with a woman who kept bees and goats, she asked questions about apiculture while watching Ludovic circulate. He appeared to know and be known by almost everyone present except her companion, who said, 'Who is that tall, dark man in the blazer and white jeans?'

'Ludovic Webb of Ramillies.'

'Oh, is *that* him? I've heard a great deal about him from my honey and milk customers, but I don't have an active social life. If I did it wouldn't be in his milieu.

I only came here tonight because Hattie was so insistent. I'm usually in bed by nine or soon after.'

'What sort of things have you heard about him?' Olivia asked.

'People have mentioned his kindness. I'd expected him to be a much older man. The fish mousse is quite delicious. Did you have some?'

'No, but I can recommend this chicken in curry sauce if you go for a refill.' Olivia forced herself to finish the chicken on her plate without looking in the direction of the broad navy blue shoulders and long white-denimed legs.

She was still in conversation with the bee-keeper, who, though talkative, seemed unlikely to mingle if left on her own, when those long legs and the well-polished loafers at the bottom of them intruded on the pattern of the oriental rug Olivia had been looking at while she listened.

'May I take away those empty plates?' Ludovic asked, smiling down at them.

Before Olivia could introduce him, the bee-keeper said, 'How kind of you, but I'm going to replenish mine. Do have my seat. I believe you two know each other, and I've just seen someone I want to have a word with.' She swept off towards the buffet, her feet shod in Greek peasant sandals worn with opaque purple tights.

'How did she know that?' he asked, taking her place.

'She asked who you were and I told her.'

'Would you like me to replenish your plate?'

'No, thank you. Where's your plate? Wouldn't you like some more?'

'I ate at home with my house-guests, whom I've now

rather churlishly deserted in order to be with you. It's rather close in here. Shall we get some fresh air?'

With irresistible aplomb, he removed the plate from her lap, adding it to a tray of plates being collected by Hattie's daily help, at the same time taking Olivia gently but firmly by the elbow and sweeping her to her feet and towards the glass door leading to the garden behind the barn.

'I don't think you'll be cold. It's very mild out tonight,' he said, as he opened it for her.

The garden was lit by lamps concealed behind shrubs and plants, giving the effect of a stage set for a drama on which the curtain had risen but no one had yet made an entrance.

'But in case you do find it chilly. . .' Ludovic continued, removing his blazer and placing it round her shoulders.

His gesture dredged up a memory of Tom stripping off his T-shirt and holding it over her head in a vain attempt to prevent her hair beings rats'-tailed by a tropical downpour which in minutes had drenched them both.

Now, in a very different context, she was filled by the same inner glow of a female in the protective care of an innately chivalrous male.

'Thank you,' she said, in a low voice. 'Why did you want to see me? Have you changed your mind about some of my proposals?'

'On the contrary, the more I study them, the more remarkable I find it that you've demonstrated such an acute grasp of the character of the house. I've spent nine years getting to know Ramillies in all its aspects. On the strength of one short visit, you seem to know it as well as I do.'

She was tempted to say that she did, to throw off the burdensome subterfuge which had served its purpose and now made her more uncomfortable each time they met. But this wasn't the time or the place. At any moment others might come into the garden. When she *did* come clean, it had to be somewhere private, where they wouldn't be disturbed.

'Do I really strike you as ruthless?' she asked, referring back to his remark with reference to Annette's ability to run a catering business.

'Aren't you?' he said, looking amused.

She was provoked into saying, 'Not nearly as ruthless as you.'

'Probably not, although I don't know what grounds you have for that assessment. I've never shown you my sterner side. Quite the reverse.'

Olivia had one hand on the lapels of his blazer, in case it should slide off her narrower shoulders on to the night-damp grass. Suddenly he captured her other hand, threading his fingers through hers and stroking the base of her thumb with his own.

'You bring out my nicer qualities, Olivia,' he told her softly.

The caressing tone sent a shiver down her spine. 'You still haven't explained why you want to talk to me.'

CHAPTER NINE

No SPECIFIC reason. I enjoy talking to you.' He lifted her hand to chest-height, drawing her round to face him. 'Almost as much as kissing you.'

'Ludovic. . .please. . . We can be seen from the gallery.'

'If anyone is looking, yes. I shouldn't think they are. They're all tucking in to the puddings.'

Reminded of Annette, she stepped back, trying to disengage her hand. 'Annette tells me you gave her a portable telephone for night-driving.'

His expression changed. He looked irritated. 'I think every woman should have one. I hope you do.'

'Yes, but tonight I'm staying here.'

'I'd rather you were staying at Ramillies. Why not come over for lunch tomorrow?'

'After neglecting them tonight, shouldn't you concentrate on your visitors?'

He was still in possession of her hand and his fingers tightened. 'You make it hard to concentrate on anything.'

As he moved closer, the look in his eyes made her catch her breath. He was determined to have her, and she wasn't sure she could resist him. . .or wanted to resist him.

At that moment the quiet of the garden was broken by a burst of sound from inside the gallery as someone else opened the door. Glancing over her head at whoever was emerging, Ludovic looked as if he might be swearing inwardly.

The three people who had intruded on their seclusion—to Olivia's mingled relief and disappointment—were strangers to her and apparently unknown to Ludovic. They were two men and a woman, whose conversation indicated that they had come outside to look at some unusual plant.

She said, 'We'd better go in and try Annette's marvellous puddings.'

'Her party puds are usually too sweet for my taste. Sugar and cream don't tempt me as much as other things,' he said, looking at her mouth.

Olivia pretended not to notice. As they reached the door, she shrugged off his blazer and gave it back to him. 'Thanks.'

'My pleasure.' He hooked a finger through the silk loop inside the collar and slung it over his shoulder. As usual, he was wearing an immaculately fresh blue cotton shirt. Before opening the door he said, 'So what about lunch tomorrow? Yes?'

She had told the Frosts she would be going back to London during the morning.

'All right. What time?'

'About twelve forty-five?'

Olivia nodded. 'Who are your house-guests?'

'A small deputation from France. Burghers who are thinking of converting a medieval castle into a set-up like Ramillies. They all speak English.'

'I shouldn't have thought it would have strengthened the *entente cordiale* to desert them so soon after dinner,' she remarked.

'I explained why it was necessary. The French are very understanding about anything involving *l'amour*.'

She was startled into looking up at him, and the look in his eyes threw her into even more confusion than his statement.

'Ludovic, dear boy, how are you? And who is this lovely creature? Introduce me forthwith.' A middle-aged man with a whisky-drinker's complexion and a smoker's breath gave her a wolfish smile.

He turned out to be a landowner, whom she remembered being referred to as a lecherous nincompoop by Rathbone when the newcomer's wife had brought a divorce suit against him.

Evidently Ludovic shared his great-uncle's opinion. He performed the requested introduction but soon afterwards led her away to the buffet where, having introduced her to some nicer people, he excused himself and went home.

The party went on till one, and it was two-fifteen before Olivia fell into bed.

Ever since Ludovic's departure, his remark about 'anything involving *l'amour*' had been going round and round in her mind.

What had he meant? *L'amour* had so many shades of meaning. Love. . .affection. . .passion. It covered everything from a lifetime of devotion to a one-night stand. Where, on the scale between the two extremes, did Ludovic's use of the word come?

She was still awake, grappling with that conundrum, when she heard the long-case clock in the gallery strike three. The chimes were a potent reminder of Ramillies where, at the age of ten, she had been entrusted with the task of winding some of the many clocks in the house.

Even if it was possible that Ludovic had fallen seriously in love with her, she had a sinking feeling that what she would tell him tomorrow would at once change his feelings towards her.

While she didn't believe Ben's allegation that Ludovic was a snob, she couldn't feel confident that, when he knew who she was, he would feel the same way about her as he did now. However that was.

She arrived at Ramillies an hour before she was bidden, explaining to the man on gate duty that she wanted to park her car and go for a walk in the park before presenting herself at the house for lunch.

'That's all right, Miss Hartley,' he said, crossing her off a list on his clip-board. 'It's a nice morning for a stroll. You'll enjoy your lunch more after a walk in the fresh air. You may run into our French visitors.'

Olivia hoped not. She wanted time to herself before the ordeal ahead. Breakfast with the Frosts had been rather trying. They had all been tired, but she thought Ben had had a hangover. He had snapped at Hattie a couple of times. No doubt she would have snapped back if there hadn't been a visitor present. Olivia had had the impression he might not be easy to live with.

Although she hadn't expected to be doing any country walking, she always kept a pair of stout-soled loafers, a waterproof and an old sweater in the boot of the car. As she changed her shoes, she thought that if the French were exploring the grounds they would most likely go in the direction of the arboretum planted in the last century by a Victorian Webb.

On that assumption, she went in the opposite direction, following a route which brought her to the crest of a hill to the east of the house. There she sat down on the grass to enjoy a favourite view which, nine years ago, she had thought she would never see again.

For a while she let herself daydream that Ludovic *was* in love with her and wanted to stay at Ramillies and share his part of it with her. But she knew it was only wishful thinking.

Probably what he wanted was another transitory affair, which would be wonderful while it lasted, but would end in heartbreak for her when he returned to his first and only lasting love—the sea.

By half-past twelve she was back at the car park, changing into the shoes which went with her cream shirt and skirt. Having combed her hair and checked her make-up, she headed for the house.

All the way down from the hill-top she had been rehearsing what to say in the tête-à-tête she hoped to have with Ludovic later. But she was still uncertain how to go about it.

An envelope with her name on it was taped to the open front door. She slit it open and found a brief handwritten message—'We'll be having aperitifs in my sitting-room.'

The French delegation consisted of two married couples and two other people, a young man and an older woman. In all, fourteen people, including Geoffrey but not Annette, sat down to luncheon in the dining-room used for formal occasions.

Seated three places from Ludovic, who was flanked by the two French wives, Olivia suspected that the original number had been twelve and that Geoffrey was a last moment addition to bring it up to fourteen including herself. Not that Ludovic would be superstitious, but he might feel that some of his guests would dislike a table of thirteen.

Before lunch, most of her conversation had been

with the formidably chic Frenchwoman whom he had introduced as the principal of an art college. Now she found herself between one of the married Frenchmen and the younger man, an architect.

The occasion would have been more enjoyable if she hadn't been preoccupied with the confrontation to come. Not that she was obliged to blow her cover today. But if not today, when? She had to declare herself before Ludovic made his move. . .whatever it might be.

Coffee was taken in the library, and by three o'clock the local guests were beginning to take their leave. Olivia had thought Ludovic was being facetious when, the night before, he had claimed to have told the French that *l'amour* was the reason he had to desert them.

But, as soon as the English guests had gone, one of the Frenchwomen said she would like to rest, a suggestion immediately seconded by the others in her party. As they said goodbye to Olivia, the same woman gave her a conspiratorial smile, which seemed to confirm that Ludovic hadn't been teasing and that *madame* felt sure Olivia was the quarry he was pursuing.

'Are you tired?' he asked, when they were alone.

She shook her head, her mouth dry.

'What time did you get to bed?'

'Not till after two, but the Frosts aren't early risers so I had a lie-in this morning.'

'What would you like to do now? Go for a stroll round the garden? Relax with the Sunday papers until it's time for tea?'

'Let's go round the garden. . .if that's all right with you?'

'Anything's all right with me. . .as long as I'm doing it with you.'

The confusing thing was that it wasn't said with the slightly exaggerated gallantry which would have made it clear that it shouldn't be taken seriously. He sounded and looked as if he meant it.

'Do many people come with a view to copying what you've done here?' she asked, to break the tension she felt zinging between them.

'Yes, there's a lot of interest. But right now I don't want to think about that side of Ramillies. For the next couple of hours let's forget our public personae and be our private selves. How do you spend your holidays?'

'Sometimes I go and stay with Tyler and Bonnie. Last year I was included in a house party at a client's mill-house in France.'

'Next month I'm going to Wales for a few days' rock-climbing. Would you like to come with me? Some women make excellent climbers.'

'Are you going with a group?'

'No, it would be just the two of us. . .a chance to get to know each other better. You don't have to decide this afternoon. Think about it.'

By this time they were in the garden, walking away from the house.

Olivia took a deep breath. 'I don't think I'd make a climber. I haven't a good head for heights.' She swung round to face the house. 'When your great-uncle bought a TV to watch the Falklands War news, I went up on the roof with the engineer who fixed the aerial. Looking over the edge made my head swim. He said it was vertigo.'

She thought it might take a while for the penny to drop.

But, after staring intently at her for five or ten seconds, Ludovic said, 'Good God! The spitfire from Costa Rica.'

She didn't correct him, surprised he should even remember it had been Central America she had flown in from that day.

'I thought there was something familiar about you the day I came to your office,' he said, his eyes still intent. 'But I thought——' He broke off, frowning. 'The first time we met you called yourself Olly Jones.'

'You assumed my surname was Jones. I wasn't George Jones's son's child. My mother was his daughter. I was named in your great-uncle's will as Olivia Jane Hartley.'

'Were you? I don't remember. You were always called Olly Jones by people in the village who'd known you. Why didn't you tell me who you were from the beginning?'

'I couldn't see any point in. . .reviving old antagonisms. The past seemed irrelevant to the matter in hand. I—I didn't anticipate that you would want to put our professional relationship on a personal footing.'

'I see,' he said slowly. 'Or do I? No, I'm damned if I do.' A deep flush of anger deepened his outdoorsman's tan and his blue eyes were suddenly dangerous. 'You've been making a monkey of me. All this time, while I——'

Suddenly he grabbed her shoulders and yanked her towards him. In full view of anyone looking out from the windows of the south front, Ludovic vented his wrath in a kiss which felt like being caught in the open by a hurricane.

For the first few moments, her response was instinctive. Somewhere, deep down inside, the primitive being at the core of her relished the conquest by powerful arms and punitive lips. Instinct, and the feeling that she deserved his anger, combined in unresisting submission to the onslaught of *force majeure*.

Then years of conditioning triggered a different reflex: the angry resentment of late twentieth-century woman at being subjected to superior male strength, even by this man. She began to struggle to free herself.

Perhaps a similar process accounted for Ludovic's reaction. The barbarian in him would have ignored her resistance. But instead of subduing her, as he could easily have done, the civilised man let her go.

Thrusting her away as abruptly as he had grabbed her, he said furiously, 'Now, I suppose, you'll accuse me of sexual harassment.'

'I could accuse you of many things,' Olivia flared back at him. 'I'd better leave before you make an even bigger exhibition of yourself.'

Stiff-backed and tight-lipped, she marched to the car park, only to realise, on reaching it, that her keys were in her bag and her bag was in the library.

Dreading another encounter, she returned to the house to fetch it. The library was empty and she saw no one, although her return and departure would have been filmed by the cameras enabling the duty security officer to monitor all the comings and goings. Ludovic had explained the complex and costly system to her, but the lenses were so unobtrusive that probably few of the students realised that Ramillies's treasures and anyone near them were under constant surveillance.

Driving back to London, Olivia forced herself to keep her mind on the road and not brood on what had happened. But as soon as she was at home it overwhelmed her. Without bothering to unpack or change, she flung herself down on her bed and lay with closed eyes, reliving those angry last moments and cursing herself for ever going back to Ramillies and being foolish enough to get involved with its owner.

If she'd had any sense, the night she'd come back from her final dinner with Mark and heard Ludovic's voice on her answering-machine, she should have written him a note to say she had too much work lined up to take on any more. Instead, driven by financial anxiety, she had messed up her personal life.

At nine o'clock, after she had written a thank-you note to Hattie and was watching the news, the telephone rang. It was the night porter.

'I've Mr Webb with me, Miss Hartley. He'd like to see you.'

Olivia tensed. What could have brought Ludovic to London on a Sunday evening? Was he angry enough to try to back out of the contract? Should she refuse to see him?

As she deliberated, she heard Ludovic say, 'Let me speak to her.' The next moment he was on the line, saying, 'Olivia, I must talk to you. There are things we have to straighten out.'

'All right. . .but give me ten minutes. I—I was just about to take a shower.'

'Call down when you're ready,' he suggested.

Eight minutes later, her house-robe replaced by jeans and a coral shirt, she rang down to say, 'You can send Mr Webb up now.'

Her final check in the mirror near her front door showed no sign of the tears which had smeared her eye make-up earlier. It wasn't like her to cry, but she had while lying on her bed. Then she had gone to the bathroom and cleaned off the smudged mascara and sponged her eyes with cold water. Now they were back to normal, as if the foolish and uncharacteristic tears had never been shed.

But she wasn't feeling normal inside herself. She knew it wouldn't take much to shatter her shaky self-possession. Probably it was stupid to see him again today. But when he had come all this way, how could she refuse?

Outwardly composed, inwardly apprehensive, she waited for the bell to ring.

When she opened the door, Ludovic was standing in the hallway with his hands in the pockets of a dun leather jacket and a vivid silk scarf coiled round his neck. It was hard to tell from his expression what sort of mood he was in.

She gestured for him to enter and he walked straight through to her living-room, where he turned to face her as she followed him.

'After you'd gone, I remembered you'd left your bag in the house. When I couldn't find it, I played back the tape on the security monitor and saw you fetching it. You looked. . .upset. I was worried about you driving back in that state.'

She had an insane desire to fling herself into his arms and burst into tears on his chest. But, in spite of his professed concern, his expression didn't suggest that an emotional reaction would be well received. There were knots of muscle moving at the angles of his jaw, suggesting anger and impatience held in control but still liable to erupt.

She said stiffly, 'You could have rung up.'

'It seemed a better idea to come and thrash this thing out.'

In an effort to normalise the situation, she said, 'Would you like some coffee?'

'Thank you.' He pulled his scarf free, stuffing it in a pocket before removing the jacket and tossing it on a chair.

She had never seen him with a noticeable five-o'-clock shadow before. The dark pattern of his beard seemed to emphasise the quintessential maleness of his face, with its taut skin and prominent bones. Only the sensual mouth and sometimes humorous eyes relieved the commanding structure of his features. But just now his lips were compressed and there was no amusement in his eyes. He looked dauntingly stern, a man in quest of explanations and apologies rather than *rapprochement*.

He followed her to the kitchen and stood in the doorway, where the top of his head was not far short of the lintel and his shoulders filled the space between the jambs in a way she had never been aware of when Mark had stood there.

He watched her setting a tray before saying, 'You said there were many accusations you could throw at me. Let's start from there.'

'I was angry. . .dredging up scores better forgotten. It's all a long time ago.'

'Scores which are better out in the open and resolved,' Ludovic corrected her.

'They can't be resolved. It's too late.'

'That statement may make sense to you. It doesn't to me. Explain yourself.'

His peremptory tone lit an angry sparkle in her eyes. 'All right, I'll spell it out. It didn't suit you to honour your great-uncle's promise to leave my grandfather the use of the lodge. So you hustled him into an institution where he was so unhappy he drank himself to death.'

'Do you really believe that?'

'It's not something I've been told. I saw it with my own eyes. I visited him every weekend. He was like a wild bird in a cage and he couldn't bear it.' Her voice quivered as she remembered those painful, despairing visits during the months of George Jones's deterioration.

For some moments Ludovic frowned at the floor in silence. Then he said quietly, 'You won't like what I'm going to tell you, but it has to be said. Your grandfather didn't take to the bottle after he left Ramillies. He had been an alcoholic for years. It's not an uncommon condition among butlers and publicans.'

'That's not true,' Olivia protested. 'He wasn't a drinker before I went away. . . At least, no more than Mr Webb.'

'I dare say *he* knocked back more than was good for his liver,' Ludovic said drily, 'but he wasn't smashed out of his mind the night burglars broke in and stole the Reynolds. I doubt if you know about that episode. It isn't likely your grandfather would have told you.'

The boiling kettle switched itself off, but Olivia made no move to pour the hot water on to the granules she'd spooned into the cups. 'The Reynolds was stolen?' she said blankly.

'Yes, and never recovered.' He stepped into the narrow kitchen and did what she was too startled and shaken to do. 'Presumably it's now in the possession of some unscrupulous collector who didn't enquire too closely into its provenance. Unfortunately, it wasn't insured.'

'When did this happen?'

'About four months before you came back. If you doubt my word, I can show you the Press-clippings. The story was crowded out of the national papers by more sensational events, but it made the front page of the local paper. "Rich Recluse Robbed of Reynolds" was one of their headlines.'

He carried the tray into the living-room, leaving Olivia, still dazed by shock, to follow.

The portrait of Lady Caroline Webb, an impoverished peer's daughter who had married a handsome commoner rich enough to have his wife's face immortalised by the brush of Sir Joshua Reynolds, the most famous artist of his day, had hung in Mr Webb's bedroom, which Olivia had seldom entered. She had only a hazy memory of a woman in eighteenth-century clothes with the house and park in the background.

'The thieves broke in through a downstairs window which had been opened for airing by the cleaner and should have been shuttered and barred by George Jones,' Ludovic continued. 'But he neglected that duty. . .and many others. A less tolerant employer would have sacked him long before the burglary.'

'You never knew your great-uncle. He wasn't an easy man to work for,' Olivia said defensively. 'Not many people would have stayed with him. We had difficulty keeping cleaners. He used to shout if they moved things. He never shouted at me, but was very snappy with Granpa sometimes.'

'Probably with reason,' said Ludovic. 'The night the

burglars broke in and trussed him up, Rathbone
shouted his head off for an hour, but Jones was out for
the count. Eventually Rathbone managed to free himself and call the police. But by then the thieves were
back in London, or wherever their base was. By the
time Jones was fit to knock back a hair of the dog, the
Reynolds was probably already out of the country.'

After pouring out the coffee, he added, 'That's only
conjecture, of course. We shall never know what
happened to it. But it's not speculation on my part
that Jones went to bed drunk that night. It's the
opinion of the police officers who handled the
enquiry.'

Olivia sank on to the sofa, feeling pole-axed. She
had had no inkling that a drama of this sort had
happened during her absence. The staff and perhaps
other residents at the place where her grandfather had
spent the interval between leaving Ramillies and being
hospitalised must have heard about it. But no one had
mentioned it to her. Perhaps they'd assumed she knew.

She remembered Mr Webb's hope that she would
abstain from drinking and smoking while she was away
from home. Had that been because he knew her
grandfather suffered from alcoholism and feared she
might be susceptible?

'You look as if you could do with something stronger
than coffee,' said Ludovic, handing her a cup and
saucer. 'Shall I get you some brandy?'

'No, no,' she said emphatically. 'I'm not a secret
tippler.'

'I never supposed you were. Don't lose your sense
of proportion because of this, Olivia. One of my
father's maxims was "never trust a teetotaller". They
usually have as many hang-ups as dipsos. One way and

another, you've had a difficult day. So have I. We'll both have a reviver.'

She watched him go to the drinks tray, open the ice-tub, find it empty and take it to the kitchen.

By the time he came back she was beginning to recover from her initial stupefaction. But it wasn't easy to adjust to this new perspective of her grandfather, not Ludovic, as the miscreant in the matter.

'If you'd told me who you were at the outset, we could have cleared this up a long time ago,' said Ludovic, dropping ice-cubes into two tumblers. 'Why did you keep your identity under wraps?'

'I needed the Ramillies contract. I didn't think I'd get it if you knew who I was. That angry letter I wrote after you sent me packing. . .'

'I tore it up,' he said, bringing the drinks to the sofa and giving one glass to her before sitting down next to her. 'Months later, when there was time to sort out the old boy's personal papers, I came across your letters to him. At first I intended to scrap them, but after I'd read a few they seemed worth preserving. They're in an archive box in the library. If you like, you can have them back. Now that you're a successful career woman, you might find a publisher for them. You were better-read than most teenagers and good at describing people and places. I sometimes wondered what had happened to you. But, from what I'd seen, you seemed eminently capable of taking care of yourself.'

'In the circumstances, I don't suppose you'd have lost much sleep if I hadn't been,' she said, avoiding his eyes. 'At the time I thought it was a disgraceful cop-out for you only to pay the balance of Granpa's overheads after he'd had most of his pension deducted. But I realise now it was actually very magnanimous.'

'I thought so too,' he said drily. 'In retrospect, I think I was probably rather unkind to you both. But you entered my life—the first time—at a difficult juncture. As a boy I'd dreamed of Ramillies. It represented stability and continuity to someone who'd never known either. For me to inherit the estate was like winning the major prize in a lottery. Or so I thought till I got there and saw the reality—a crumbling old house, no money, and one of its major assets wafted out of the window.'

'I didn't know you'd dreamed about Ramillies. You didn't sound as if you had. Tyler Westmacott had the impression you were itching to get back to the sea.'

'I do miss the sea. It's in my blood,' he agreed. 'But it's not the right life for a family man, which is how I see my future.'

'Because you feel an obligation to Ramillies?'

'No, because I want a wife and children. Because——'

He broke off at the sound of a key being inserted in her front door.

Had she been alone, Olivia would have been alarmed, assuming that someone was entering illegally. With Ludovic near her, she felt only puzzlement.

They heard the door open, then a man's voice saying, 'Olivia?'

She stifled a gasp of dismay. Because he had seldom used it, she had forgotten Mark had a key to the flat. But why had he come without warning? And tonight of all nights?

The next moment he came into view, his face reflecting her feelings when he saw she wasn't alone.

'Mark. . . What are you doing here?'

'I—I needed to see you. . .to talk. As the porter wasn't around, I came straight up. I expected to find you working.'

Ludovic had risen to his feet. 'You're Mark Marton. I've seen you on TV. My name is Ludovic Webb. I don't suppose Olivia has mentioned me. She hasn't mentioned you. I'm merely a client of her business. Her connection with you is, I gather, rather more intimate.'

He didn't offer his hand and the look on his face wasn't friendly.

'Olivia and I are old friends,' Mark answered stiffly.

Ludovic lifted an eyebrow. 'But only in her present incarnation as the successful Miss Hartley? You never knew her as Olly?'

'Olly?' Mark looked blank.

'I must be going.' Ludovic turned to Olivia. 'I thought we had things straightened out, but it seems we hadn't. Don't bother to see me out. Goodnight. Goodnight, Marton.'

She was tempted to beg him to wait, to try to explain that things weren't the way they must look. But with Mark standing by it was futile to attempt it. Anyway, she didn't know for certain what Ludovic had been about to say when they'd heard the key scratch in the lock.

What she had *hoped* he might say could be mere wishful thinking.

CHAPTER TEN

LUDOVIC didn't slam the door, but she had the feeling he would have liked to. She had seen that angry glitter in his eyes earlier today. It had been there again as he said goodnight.

'Mark, what possessed you to burst in on me like that?' she said despairingly.

'I'm sorry. I didn't expect it to be inconvenient. Yesterday my help found the key to your door in the pocket of a suit I'd put out to go to the cleaners. Rather than posting it to you, I thought I'd bring it round. The fact is. . . Well, actually. . .'

His usual fluency seemed to have deserted him. He looked at her uncertainly.

'I know I can't expect you to be glad to see me when I was the one who suggested we separate. But it seemed the only way to make you realise there's more to life than a career. I thought you would miss me, Olivia. I've missed you. I want you back.'

She was too upset to deal gently with him. 'You can't be serious! Your arrogance takes my breath away. So there's more to life than a career, is there? But that doesn't mean you'd give up *your* career, does it? Not likely! What you mean is, you hoped *I* would miss you enough to sacrifice *my* career. Well, I'm sorry, I haven't. There *is* one man I'd sacrifice everything for. But, thanks to you, he's just walked out of here thinking. . .thinking the worst.'

It took Mark at least half a minute to digest this

outburst. 'You can't be in love with this Webb chap. You haven't known him long enough.'

'I met him nine years ago. I realise now the reason I was so angry with him was because I had taken one look and fallen in love with him. All these years I've been telling myself I hated his guts. And part of me did. But once you've laid eyes on Ludovic, nobody else ever quite matches up.'

'You mean, all the time you were with me, you were thinking about him?' Mark said indignantly.

'No, it wasn't like that. I'd put him out of my mind. . .my conscious mind. It wasn't until the night you sent me packing that I heard from him again. I came home and found a message from him on my answering-machine. While I was with you, I really hoped it would work out for us. But it didn't and it never could. Your career *does* come first in your life. Any time there was a three-line whip demanding your attendance at the House, you'd be there, Mark. . .no matter what was happening in your private life. You'd rather upset your wife than flout the sacred commands of the party whips. It's they who set your priorities. But if Ludovic loved a woman, he'd let Ramillies burn to the ground if she needed him somewhere else.'

He said angrily, 'So how come he's walked out now? What does he want? A virgin? He's going to have a long search.'

'From the fact that you have a key, he probably thinks we're still on intimate terms,' she said dully. 'It's not an unreasonable conclusion when a man has access to a woman's flat.'

'What did he mean about my not knowing you as Olly?'

'That's what I used to be called a long time ago. It's the name I gave him the first time we met.'

'When you had a teenage crush on him,' was his acid comment.

'When I thought I disliked him,' she corrected. 'Now I know more about him, and I realise he isn't at all the way I thought he was.'

Mark started to pace the room, a habit of his when expounding some political issue on which he had strong feelings. But this time he paced in silence, unconsciously chewing his lips—a mannerism he had been instructed to drop by a coach who taught Members of Parliament how to perform to advantage when they appeared on TV.

After some moments, he said, 'What do you want me to do? Phone him and tell him there isn't anything between us. . .hasn't been for some time?'

The offer surprised and touched her. Perhaps he really did love her if he was prepared to go to that length for her.

She shook her head. 'I'll tell him myself. . .the next time I go to Ramillies.'

Mark came to where she was standing and put his hands on her shoulders. 'Even if he believes you, I don't think it's going to turn out the way you want, Olivia,' he said gravely. 'I knew his name rang a bell and now I've made the connection. He's the man who turned his ancestral home into one of the most successful independent colleges in the country.'

'It wasn't his ancestral home in the usual sense. He'd never been there until it was left to him.'

'Maybe so, but I'd bet he was always sure of his top dog status. I've met his type before. They don't

like people like me—achievers with brains but no
background—and they don't like assertive women.'

'I don't agree. The stronger a man is, the less he
minds strength in women. It's the men who *aren't* sure
of themselves who resent women's aspirations.' Feeling emotionally drained, wanting to be on her own,
she said, 'Anyway, whatever happens, it's over
between us, Mark. You made the right decision the
night you broke it off. Our relationship had been
winding down for some time. I don't think you really
want me back. It's a case of everyone needing someone. . .and you just haven't found the right person
yet. I'm sure you will, if you keep looking. You're a
highly eligible man. You'll be in the Cabinet by the
time you're forty.'

'I hope so.'

As always, the thought of the political summits he
planned to climb brought the light of zeal to his eyes.

Their parting, like the previous one, was amicable.
Olivia felt sure she needn't lose any sleep over Mark.
Power and prestige would always be his most important goals, with family life playing a secondary part in
his scheme.

She had thought her career was of first importance
to her, but now she knew that all she'd achieved so
far, and everything she might achieve in the next thirty
or forty years, would not be enough to fulfil her
completely.

Only one person could do that, and tonight she was
still as unsure how he felt about her as she had been
yesterday.

That he'd followed her to London was promising.
But what was in his mind now, after finding out that
she had a close and apparently on-going relationship

with a man he had once described as a 'posturing idiot'?

If Ludovic thought back to that conversation, he would probably feel she had misled him then, implying that Mark was a casual acquaintance, not someone who had, for a time, been important to her.

She was woken by the telephone.

'Are you alone?'

'I've been alone since shortly after you left here.'

'Because Marton was angry at finding me there?'

She had rehearsed this conversation a dozen times in the small hours, but had seen it happening at Ramillies, not down the line at seven o'clock in the morning, with her brain still foggy from sleep.

'Mark and I split up the night you left a message for me to call you. I haven't seen him since then. I shan't be seeing him again. We were. . .involved for three years, but we never actually lived together.' She wished she could see Ludovic's face and gauge his reaction. Not that his face ever gave much away. 'Our lives didn't mesh very well. I'm not politically-minded and he isn't much interested in my field,' she concluded.

There was a pause before he answered, 'The last time I wanted to smash someone's teeth down his throat was in my salad days. On that occasion the other guy was asking for trouble. Marton wasn't. You're upsetting my equilibrium. I think we need to discuss the situation further. Will you have breakfast with me?'

'Where are you?'

'At the Nabob. . . Or we could go to Richoux's, if you'd rather.'

Richoux's, with its long-skirted waitresses, was a popular Mayfair patisserie where affluent Londoners went to have a breakfast or brunch. She had once taken Mark to Richoux's, although, if he went out for breakfast, he preferred the Savoy, where he was likely to see and be seen by other men of influence.

'I'll come to the club. What time?'

'The sooner the better. I've been awake since five.'

'I'll be there in an hour.'

'I'll be waiting.' He rang off.

Olivia jumped out of bed, shedding her nightie on the way to the shower. Surely, surely this had to mean he felt the same way as she did? Why else had he felt an urge to punch Mark in the teeth?

It took her twenty-five minutes to shower, wash her hair and dry it. Ten minutes to do her face. Seven minutes to dress in new dark blue jeans and a sea-green silk shirt bought in Paris and put by for a special occasion. This, unquestionably, was it.

She entered the club fifty-six minutes after Ludovic's call.

The porter, advised of her arrival, said, 'Good morning, Miss Hartley. You'll find Mr Webb on the terrace. Go to the end of the corridor and you'll see the terrace to your left.'

'Thank you.' Her heart beating fast, she followed his directions.

The glass doors leading into the garden at the back of the building were already open to the warmth of an early heat-wave. As she stepped through them, and glanced right and left, she saw a familiar pair of long legs, the ankle of one resting on the knee of the other.

Ludovic's head and body were screened by the business section of a broadsheet.

The relaxation of his posture made her feel their rendezvous couldn't be as crucial to his well-being as it was to hers. Perhaps their objectives were different; hers being more serious and permanent than what he had in mind for them.

Filled with misgivings, she said, 'Good morning.'

The alacrity with which he cast the paper aside and spang up to greet her was reassuring.

'Olivia!' In a few strides he was beside her, taking her hands in his. 'You look wonderful. You must have slept much better than I did.'

Suddenly she felt wonderful. The warmth she saw in his eyes gave her hope that today it was going to come right between them.

'Why was that?' she asked.

'You know why. You must know by now.' His hands tightened over hers. 'I want you to come back to Ramillies. Even if we have to share it with hundreds of people, it's where we both belong. You love it as much as I do. But I love you even more. The reason I couldn't sleep last night was because I wasn't sure what you'd say if I asked you to marry me. I'm asking you now, Olivia. What *do* you say?'

'I—I was afraid you only wanted to have an affair with me,' she told him. 'But I wanted you to love me as much as I love you, Ludovic.'

'As I do. . .as I always will.' He released her hands, but only to put his arms round her and draw her against him. 'It's taken a long time to find you. The first time we met you were too young and I had a millstone round my neck. . .or so it seemed at the time. But now we're both ready to start the best part of our lives. . .together.'

As she laid her hands on his chest and the glow in her eyes showed clearly how much his tender words meant to her, Ludovic bent his head and kissed her consenting mouth.

It was the first time they had kissed without Olivia being inwardly torn by conflicting loyalties. Now that constraint had gone. She slid her arms round his neck and clung with joyful abandon.

It was Ludovic who, some time later, put her gently away from him saying, with a rueful grin. 'This would have to happen on a Monday morning. I expect you're going to tell me you have a raft of engagements which have priority over the celebration of *our* engagement.'

'Oh, dear. . .yes, I do,' she said, regretfully coming down to earth. 'But the last one's at three. From four o'clock on, I'm all yours.'

His eyes glinted. 'May I take that literally?'

'If you wish.'

'It's been at the top of my list for some time.'

'Mine too,' she admitted. 'Even when I thought badly of you, I couldn't help longing for you to make love to me.'

'When you look at me like that, I'm tempted to whisk you upstairs,' he said, smiling. 'But I think we had better defer that pleasure until tonight and content ourselves with having our first breakfast together.'

'We had breakfast together when I came to Ramillies,' she reminded him.

'But not by ourselves, and you were being very stand-offish because I had dared to kiss you the night before. Wait here, and I'll see if I can persuade them to serve breakfast outside.'

Presently, strolling round the club's garden while a table was laid for them, he said, 'What sort of wedding would you like? Small and private would suit me, but I think your American friends and your staff would be disappointed if we didn't invite them.'

'And your staff,' said Olivia. 'Except Annette. She's going to be upset, Ludovic. She's in love with you. Were you. . .close, at one time?'

He shook his head. 'It could have happened, before I met you, but it didn't. Annette's used to being a wife. She wouldn't be happy in a short-term liaison and I never saw her as a life-time companion and the mistress of Ramillies.'

'I'm surprised you see me in that role. If it ever gets out who I am—the drunken butler's granddaughter— it could be embarrassing for you.'

To her surprise, he put a hand on her shoulder and turned her to face him, momentarily stern. 'That's like saying that I'm the grandson of a dissolute wastrel who had to be paid to stay away. We aren't defined by our parents or grandparents, or the circumstances in which we started life. We make our own identities, and you've done a good job with yours. Any man would be proud to have someone as lovely and talented as you are as his wife, Olivia.'

He was waiting for her in the ground floor reception area when she finished work that afternoon.

'It's almost impossible to concentrate when you've just discovered what it's like to be truly, totally happy,' she told him, as they strolled down Walton Street to the meter where he had parked his car.

Ludovic hadn't embraced her in front of the recep- tionist. Now he put his arm round her waist and bent to kiss her cheek. 'I know. It's been the same for me. After organising tonight's unofficial honeymoon and checking out some possibilities for the official one, I've also spent the day checking my watch through the interminably slow count-down to four o'clock.'

'Where are we going tonight?'

'To a country hotel, about an hour's run from London, where I'm assured we'll be extremely comfortable and well-fed.'

'We'll have to stop off at my flat so that I can quickly pack an overnight case,' she said, as they reached the car.

'Not necessary,' Ludovic stooped to unlock the passenger door. 'I went to Harvey Nichols and picked up everything I thought you might need. It's all in a bag in the boot.'

On the way out of London, she said, 'There's so much I don't know about your life before you came to Ramillies.'

He took his eyes off the road to give her a smiling glance. 'It was only a warm-up. The real action began at Ramillies. In the unlikely event that anyone ever wants to write my biography, I'll insist they start the day I saw the house and, soon afterwards, met my future wife. . .but failed at the time to recognise her.'

'My instincts recognised you,' Olivia confessed. 'But I didn't want to hear what they were telling me. Even if you hadn't seemed like a usurper to me, I would never have thought I could interest you. The fact is I didn't. . .then. You saw me as merely a nuisance.'

'A rather appealing nuisance,' Ludovic responded. 'But you're right. You did seem very young, and I wasn't into nymphets.'

'Who was the girl you told me about? The one who knew how to handle a lecherous skipper?'

This time his glance was puzzled. Clearly, whoever she had been, she didn't have a place in the foreground of his memory now.

It was only after Olivia had reminded him of that first day's conversation about crewing that he said, 'That was Inge. Like me, she grew up on a boat. As she was nearly my height, in foul-weather gear she could be mistaken for a man. Anyone who made an unwelcome pass at Inge was asking for trouble.' His mouth twitched. 'She wouldn't remonstrate with them. She'd clout them.'

'Are you speaking from experience or hearsay?'

'When I was sixteen, Inge was twenty. She gave me my first tutorials in female behaviour. I hadn't had much to do with women up to that point. It's not a field a man can ever hope to master, but I felt I was reasonably *au fait*—until I met you.'

'Were you in love with her?'

'I thought so. . .twenty years ago. Who was your first love?'

'A boy called Kiwi.'

'Did knowing him predispose you to like all New Zealanders?'

'Yes, it did. I haven't known many. But he was so nice, I've always felt warmly towards them.'

'I feel the same way about Scandinavians. The last I heard of Inge, she had married the American owner of a sailing school in the Virgin Islands. I'd guess that by now she's the mother of a large, almost grown-up family, but we haven't kept in touch. Do you know what happened to Kiwi?'

'We wrote to each other for a while, then it dwindled

to Christmas cards. The last one said he was getting married to a girl he'd grown up with. The next year I didn't receive one or send one. I doubt if we'd recognise each other if we met in the street.'

The road being clear now, he reached out to take her hand. 'I'm glad something good happened to you while you were overseas. It must have been lonely at Ramillies when you were growing up. Two old men, however fond of you they were, are no substitute for parents and brothers and sisters.'

'I wasn't unhappy. I grew up with my head full of dreams of someone wonderful coming to carry me off to a life of unalloyed bliss,' she confessed with a smile. 'But when he arrived he seemed more like the Demon King than a knight in shining armour.'

Ludovic laughed, but his tone was serious as he answered, 'I can't promise you unalloyed bliss, my love, but I know the best part of *my* life is starting today. Whatever ups and downs the future holds for us, sharing them will make the best things better and the worst things easier.'

'Just to hear you call me "my love" is wonderful to me,' she said softly.

His fingers tightened over hers before heavier traffic ahead made him release her hand to concentrate on driving.

Their destination was a small Tudor manor-house where, having parked the car, Ludovic took from the boot the grip containing his own overnight kit and the bag he had bought for her. It was a stylish roll-bag, made from a colourful kelim, with expensive leather reinforcements and a strap he would have slung over his shoulder if a shirt-sleeved youth in a baize apron had not appeared to take charge of their light luggage.

On the wall behind the reception desk an array of awards and badges given by the most exclusive travel and *haute cuisine* organisations testified to the standard of comfort they could expect from the hotel. But Olivia wouldn't have cared if they had been spending the night at the most basic of bed and breakfast establishments.

All that mattered to her was that tonight she would sleep in Ludovic's arms, and that very soon she would cease to be Olivia Hartley, except in her professional life, and would become Olivia Webb. . .Mrs Ludovic Webb. . .and, by the time she was forty, the mother of several new Webbs.

For once paying little attention to her surroundings, she stood by while Ludovic registered and then followed the porter upstairs to a spacious room overlooking a rose-garden.

Ludovic was aware that she was in a world of her own. There was a twinkle in his eyes as he said, 'I thought we'd postpone the champagne until later. There's some tea coming up. After being in London all day, I need a shower. . .and a shave,' he added, running a hand over his jaw. 'Here's the key to your bag.'

Moments later, after taking a wet-pack from his grip, he disappeared into the bathroom.

Curious to discover what the roll-bag contained, Olivia fitted the key into the miniature padlock securing the bag's zip-fastener. The many gift-wrapped parcels inside the bag reminded her of Christmas stockings filled for her by her grandfather and Ludovic's great-uncle. Except that their wrapping paper had come from the village shop and been fastened with clear Sellotape, and these packages had the more sophisticated presentation of London's most chic fashion store.

As a child she had always opened her presents carefully, smoothing and folding the paper. She did the same now, while from the bathroom came the buzz of an electric razor.

As well as practical necessities, the bag contained many non-essentials which had taken Ludovic's fancy. He had bought her a scarlet pen, an amusing note-book, a taffeta bow on a comb, gold kid mules, French scent, numerous luxurious toiletries and, swathed in layers of tissue, a nightgown of ivory satin and a matching robe piped and sashed with apricot silk. It was so simple and elegant compared to the black lace fripperies which seemed to be many men's idea of alluring nightclothes that she thought how lucky she was to love a man whose presents could be worn with real pleasure.

The tea-tray had arrived and she was sitting by the window when Ludovic reappeared with a bath-towel wrapped round his hips. It was the first time she had seen the full splendour of his shoulders and chest, and the sight made her catch her breath.

'Shall I run a bath for you?'

'Yes, please.' The glimpse she had of his back view was even more exciting: supple muscles shifting and sliding under the lightly tanned skin like a stream running over smooth rocks. Her hands were a little unsteady as she filled a cup for him.

When, leaving the water running, he joined her by the window, she said, 'I feel as if it's my birthday. . . all those lovely presents. Thank you, Ludovic. I wish I had something for you, but I didn't have time. . .'

'I have the present I want.' His blue eyes gleamed.

'The question is, shall I unwrap you. . .or let you finish your tea?'

Olivia gave a soft laugh. 'Only a *very* old lady could concentrate on afternoon tea with you standing there looking. . .' As there didn't seem to be a word to describe how wonderful he looked to her, she finished the sentence with a gesture.

He sat down in the opposite chair, beckoning her to join him. As she perched on his lap, he captured her hand and carried it up to his face, sliding it slowly down the side of his cheeks which, shaved a few minutes before, felt sensuously smooth and cool. But when he moved her hand to cover his mouth his lips were warm against her palm, and his other hand was gently but firmly persuading her to lean closer.

Her voice a husky murmur, Olivia said, 'The bath. . .it could overflow.'

'It's a big bath and the taps aren't full on.' His voice had deepened to a caressing growl. 'Kiss me again the way you did this morning.'

Relaxing against his shoulder, lifting her face to his, she saw in his eyes the fierce gleam of his hunger for her. Then she closed her own eyes and did as he had told her.

It was mid-evening when they joined the other people staying at the hotel in the wood-panelled dining-room. Although she was wearing the same clothes she had arrived in, inwardly Olivia felt a totally different person.

The deep satisfaction and joy she had always found in her work was suddenly true of her private life. Upstairs, in Ludovic's arms, everything she had dreamed of had, at long last, come true.

As they were shown to a table she glanced at the other diners, and felt sorry for those who were sharing a meal in glum silence or talking but not making eye-contact with their companions.

When they had chosen their meal, Ludovic said, 'After dinner, you'd better call Bonnie and find out how soon they can come over for the wedding. Is there somewhere you'd specially like to go for our honeymoon?'

Olivia shook her head. 'I don't know the world as well as you do. You decide. Wherever we go will be heaven.'

She had a sudden memory of the first time they had dined together and how, speaking of his parents, Ludovic had remarked that they had mated for life, adding 'as a few lucky people still do'.

It had been her first intimation that her original assessment might have been wrong. Now she had a much stronger conviction that he and she had also mated for life; that today was only the beginning. . .

A year's supply of Mills & Boon Romances—absolutely FREE!

Would you like to win a year's supply of heartwarming and passionate romances? Well, you can and they're FREE! Simply complete the wordsearch puzzle below and send it to us by 30th June 1996. The first 5 correct entries picked after the closing date will win a years supply of Mills & Boon Romances (six books every month—worth over £100). What could be easier?

READER SERVICE
ROMANCE
RESIST
HEART
MEMORIES
PAGES
KISS
SPINE
TEMPTATION
LOVE
COLLECTION
ROSES
PACK
PARCEL
TITLES
DREAMS
COUPLE
SPECIAL EDITION
EMOTION
DESIRE
SILHOUETTE
MOODS
PASSION

M	E	R	O	W	A	L	R	L	M	S	P	C	O	S
	O		E	C	I	V	R	E	S	R	E	D	A	E	R
R	O				E		O	S	M	A	E	R	D	S
O	D	H	E	A	R	T		S		S		S	E	L	T	I	T
M	S			S		E		M	E	M	O	R	I	E	S	S
A	E			C	G			S	A		C			E	W
N	P	T		A		E	K		W		O	I		W
C	E		T	P	K	I	S	S	C			L	T	T	O
E			E		H		A	E	V	O	L		E	N	N
	A	E		U		M		P	R		T	E	I	M	O	E
	E	N		L	O			L	I		S	C		P	I	O
S	L	I			H	A		S		I	T		T	S	A
	P	P	A	R	C	E	L	N	E		S	I		A	S	Z
	U	S	D	B			I	D		E	O		T	A	I
O	O		O	N			B	S		R	N		I	P	S
	C		E	N	N	A	M	T	R	R	L	G	N	O	L	T
	O		E	M	O	T	I	O	N			O	N	N	I
N	O	I	T	I	D	E	L	A	I	C	E	P	S	K

Please turn over for details of how to enter...

How to enter

Hidden in the grid are words which relate to our books and romance. You'll find the list overleaf and they can be read backwards, forwards, up, down or diagonally. As you find each word, circle it or put a line through it.

When you have found all the words, don't forget to fill in your name and address in the space provided below and pop this page into an envelope (you don't need a stamp) and post it today. Hurry—competition ends 30th June 1996.

Mills & Boon Wordsearch
FREEPOST
Croydon
Surrey
CR9 3WZ

Are you a Reader Service Subscriber? Yes ❑   No ❑

Ms/Mrs/Miss/Mr _____

Address _____

_____

_____ Postcode _____

One application per household.

You may be mailed with other offers from other reputable companies as a result of this application. If you would prefer not to receive such offers, please tick box. ❑

COMP295
F